M000214285

Edoardo Albert is a writer of Sri Lankan and Italian descent based in London. He has written a number of full length novels, as well as shorter stories for publications ranging from *Daily Science Fiction* to *Ancient Paths*. He has written features for papers and magazines including *Time Out*, *Sunday Times* and *History Today*

Conrad Monk and the Great Heathen Army

Edoardo Albert

LUME BOOKS

LUME BOOKS

First published in 2019 by Lume Books
85-87 Borough High Street,
London, SE1 1NH

ISBN 978-1-83901-162-7

www.lumebooks.co.uk

Acknowledgements

It's a well-worn truism that no book is written alone but it's just as true that a book withers and dies without readers. So my first, and greatest, thanks are extended to you for reading the adventures of Conrad Monk. If you have the chance, I'd be delighted to learn what you think: you can contact me via my website, on Facebook, or Twitter – addresses are cited below. If you've enjoyed Conrad's adventures (or even if you haven't and you want to warn off other people!), then a review, which only need be a few words, on Amazon or Goodreads would be very helpful.

Many people have helped in the writing and production of this book. I particularly want to thank my editor at Lume Books, Alice Rees, who has been unfailingly enthusiastic for the story and remarkably insightful with her criticisms – it is a much better book for her input. Cate Bickmore, who proofread the manuscript, spotted many small errors and one real howler – thank you! I'd also like to thank the rest of the staff at Lume Books for their support and help: it's a tight, smart outfit.

My wife and children nobly put up with me while I wrote the story. Due to various scheduling difficulties, I ended up writing most of the story while we were visiting family and friends in Sri Lanka. Thus, my wife, Harriet, frequently found herself asked to switch from coping with prickly heat and mosquitoes to commenting on the plausibility of Conrad escaping the patrols of the Great Heathen Army in England in winter time. That she did so is testament to her forbearance.

www.edoardoalbert.com
www.facebook.com/EdoardoAlbert.writer
@EdoardoAlbert

Glossary of place names

Early Medieval name	Modern name
Beodricesworth	Bury St Edmunds
Dubhlinn	Dublin
Exanceaster	Exeter
Fulanham	Fulham
Lun	Lynn
Medeshamstede	Peterborough
Moul	Moulsford
Readingum	Reading
Rohesia's Cross	Royston
Stane	Staines
Twicanhom	Twickenham
Wellingaford	Wallingford

Chapter 1

"Bloody Danes."

I looked to the man crouched beside me.

"Bloody, bloody Danes," Brother Odo muttered again, staring through the slats of the sty.

"Yes, they are," I hissed. "And it'll be our blood they'll be covered with if you don't shut up."

Brother Odo turned terror struck eyes towards me. "Where did they come from?"

"The Danes? Where do you think?" I squinted back out through the slats. "Idiot."

So far, the Danes — a raiding party from the Great Heathen Army that had afflicted our land for the last five years — were busy ransacking the church and the refectory, but I knew that sooner or later they would turn their attention to the monastery's other buildings. In the sty I hoped we might escape detection; but the Danes have a nose for gold that's as good as a pig's for acorns, and they'd happily sift through farmyards of manure for an arm ring. Unless help arrived soon, they would find me. I glanced at Brother Odo. Find *us*.

A scream came from behind the church.

"Is that — do you think that's — is it Emma?" asked Brother Odo, grabbing my arm, his face pale and white. Emma was the smith's daughter, a girl whose laughter and sidelong glances had made more than one of the novices blush and drop his practice stylus.

"Either that or they're mounting a sow."

Brother Odo's face paled even further, but his lips sealed in determination. He began to get up.

"I must go to her," he said.

"What?" I made a grab for him. The fool was actually going to go out there. "Wait."

But Brother Odo pushed my hand away.

"Get down," I hissed. "They'll kill you."

"We've got to do *something*," he said, his face lit up with the sort of determination that turns men into heroes. Or martyrs.

"We will do something," I said desperately. "I've got a plan. Just get down, will you."

I thought Brother Odo was going to listen. But then, Emma screamed again.

I scuttled after him on hands and knees and grabbed his ankle. Brother Odo fell forward, winding himself, and I hauled my gasping catch back into cover.

The screaming had stopped now.

"Were you trying to get us both killed?" I whispered.

"I — I must go to her," Brother Odo moaned.

"There's nothing you can do for her now," I said. "She's either dead, or they've taken her to the slave pens."

Brother Odo looked at me, and his face cracked.

"Why does God allow this?"

"Ask the bloody abbot," I answered. "He's the one who said they wouldn't come this way. I told him we should get away while there was still time."

"Yes, I remember, you did." Brother Odo grimaced. "I saw him take the brothers down into the hiding place. If the Danes don't find us, we can ask him — they'll never find him there."

I glanced at Brother Odo. "The hiding place?"

"The abbot ordered it dug, before you came to our house, when we heard the news of the Great Army. A place of sanctuary. To store the abbey's treasures and a hiding place should the Danes come."

"Why aren't *we* there?"

"When the alarm went up, I saw you were over here, by the animal pens. I came to get you, but by then, the Danes were everywhere. All we could do was hide."

"You mean, you came to save me?" I asked.

"Yes," said Brother Odo. He looked at me as if it was the most natural thing in the world. "Of course."

"I'll never forget," I said. I looked at Brother Odo's plain face, shining with the selfless goodness that would sacrifice its own chance of safety for the sake of warning another. "I'll never forget…" I repeated and added, in the hiding place of my thoughts, …*that you're a complete idiot.*

I smiled the sort of smile that invites a confidence for a confidence. "Where's the hiding place? Perhaps we can get to it."

But Brother Odo shook his head. "It's too far; the abbot had it dug into the bank by the writing huts."

My smile disappeared. The writing huts were right over on the far side of the monastery. We'd have to get past all the Danes in order to reach the hiding place.

"I've been here near six months and I've never seen it. It must be well hidden."

11

"It is," said Brother Odo. "Abbot Flory had the entrance dug where the thorn hedge on the bank is thickest, and then planted more hawthorns after it was finished. I'm surprised he never showed it to you — it is a wonder."

I was about to answer when I glanced through the slats.

"Down."

I pushed Brother Odo flat, burying his cheek in pig slurry, while I peered through the gap.

A Dane, staggering from the effects of the pitcher of ale he was drinking, was stumbling towards us. He'd slung his shield over his shoulder, but he was still carrying his axe.

I hate axes.

I pulled Brother Odo's face up out of the slurry.

"Go!" I hissed. "I'll distract him."

Gathering his habit up round his bony shanks, Brother Odo started crawling as fast as his thin legs and arms could move him. He was crawling so quickly that he did not look round to see what sort of distraction I was providing to cover his escape.

Which was just as well, because I wasn't providing the distraction. Brother Odo was.

The Dane, staggering but still on his feet, was by now barely ten feet from the sty. He raised the pitcher to his face and almost found his mouth. Ale soaked his tunic. The Dane tried again, finding his mouth this time. He peered, with the bleary, pig eyes of the angry drunk, into the empty pitcher, then threw it away and looked around for something else to drink.

Christ's teeth, was he blind?

"Hey!"

No, he wasn't.

I heard him yell for Brother Odo to stop. I was lying as flat and as still as it's possible to lie in six inches of pig slurry while still hazarding an occasional breath.

The Dane broke into a stumbling run. The sty wasn't high, but it was far easier to run round it than to attempt to vault the fence. Unfortunately, I had not counted on the Dane being so drunk that he did not see the sty. He didn't even attempt to jump the fence. He just ran into it and fell over.

On top of me.

"Don't hurt me, don't hurt me," I gibbered.

But I slowly realised that the Dane was not getting up. He was not moving at all. I poked his leg.

Nothing.

Then I saw the stone near his forehead, and the way small mud bubbles foamed round his mouth.

Falling over, he'd hit his head and knocked himself out.

Then, he stirred. His hand twitched. Just beyond its reach was the haft of the man's axe.

The Dane stirred again.

I threw myself across him, putting all my weight upon his head and pushing his face back down into the slurry.

Even unconscious, the Dane struggled, but soon the bubbles stopped, as did the struggling. I rolled off him, gasping.

"Brother Conrad, are you all right?"

It was Brother Odo, crawling back into the sty.

"God's teeth! What are you doing here?" If it had been me, I would have been half way to Wessex by now.

"I saw the Dane had seen you." Brother Odo suddenly looked stricken. "I wanted to run and leave you, I even started climbing over the bank,

13

but then I thought, what would Brother Conrad do?" He looked shyly at me. "Then it became clear what I should do." He turned to the Dane. "But of course, you didn't need my help. I should have known a great warrior like you could deal with a single Dane."

"Yes. Of course," I said.

"They say, even when a warrior lays down his sword for the sake of the Lord, he never forgets."

"Who says that?"

"Everyone," said Brother Odo.

"Yes," I nodded. "They're right."

"But now we must pray for him," said Brother Odo.

"Yes," I said. Then I added, "What?" when I realised what he had said.

"We must pray for him," said Brother Odo.

"He's a heathen," I said. "A heathen from the Great Heathen Army, who has just been pillaging a monastery. How much more heathen can you get?"

"Mayhap our prayers might save his soul from the judgement that awaits. Did not Our Lord Himself pray to the Father that those who condemned him might be spared?" Brother Odo signed himself and bent over the dead Dane, whispering the prayers for the dead and, as he did so, he wiped the muck away from the man's face.

For my part, I turned to look through the slats of the sty again.

The Danes were still ransacking the church, turning out whatever they could find and laying it on the ground in front of the building, while any of the monastery servants and monks they found were herded into the slave pens and chained together.

It was a surprisingly small pile of treasure.

Medeshamstede Abbey was wealthy. That was one of the things that made my enforced life here bearable. The table was rich, the beds were comfortable and there were plenty of servants to do the work, while the abbey church was filled with gifts of gold and cloth and ivory. And books.

Lots and lots of books. There must have been at least twelve in church and chapter house, and those richly covered and bound. There was one in particular that would have made the Danes' trip to our monastery worthwhile on its own: the Gospel Book. Nearly three hundred pages of milk-white vellum. But that's not what would attract the attention of a Dane. No, it was the book's binding: the gold of the clasps, the garnets and emeralds that studded the cover. It was a book bound with the price of a kingdom, and every time the abbot held it up before the choir of monks in the church I felt the gold lust glow in me. Any moment I expected to see a Dane emerge from the church, holding the book triumphantly aloft, but no one did.

"Looks like the Danes are stealing from the Danes," I whispered to Brother Odo, "and keeping the monastery's gold for themselves."

He came to see, putting his face to the gap in the slats. "Oh, you're wondering where the treasures are?" Brother Odo turned to me and smiled. "Abbot Flory hid them. When he heard warning that the Danes were coming."

I turned to Brother Odo. "You're saying that the abbot knew that the Danes were coming, but rather than evacuate the monastery and get us all to safety, he chose to save the monastery's gold?"

"Oh, not its gold," said Brother Odo. "Some of that he left in the church for the Danes to find, that they might be quickly satisfied and move on. But he saved our *real* treasure of course."

"What treasure?" I asked.

"The Book," said Brother Odo. "The Book of Life. He sent that, in the night, with Brother Gadd, Brother Chad and Brother Ræd, to King Edmund at *Beodricesworth*. After all, the Danes spent a year in the kingdom of the East Angles and did not lay the kingdom waste, so the Book will be safe there."

"So, the abbot saved the book, but left us to face the Danes?"

Brother Odo looked at me as if it was obvious. "Of course. It is the Book of Life."

"And we're all going to die to save it?"

"God willing," said Brother Odo.

The memory of the Gospel Book raised high in the church, its gold and garnet binding glowing as if it really was on fire with new life, came back to me. That book had had the treasures of three kingdoms, East Anglia, Mercia and Wessex, lavished upon it and Abbot Flory had sent it out into the world with only brothers Gadd, Chad and Ræd to guard it. Perhaps he thought the rhyming of their names would protect them.

The world beyond the monastery was a dangerous and unpredictable place. Three monks travelling alone through it might meet any number of accidents...

I just had to survive long enough to save the Book when the 'accident' happened.

I looked through the slats again. The first part of my plan — to survive — looked as if it was going to be the most difficult. I could see the chief of the Danes, their earl, standing in front of the church beside the meagre pile of treasure his men had found. Even from where I was, I could tell he was not pleased. As I watched, I saw him give orders to the men around him, gesturing over the monastery's grounds; he was telling them to search everywhere. Sooner or later, the Danes would check the sty where we were hiding and find not just me, but also the dead Dane. Death then would be the best I might hope for.

What could I do?

I glanced at Brother Odo. He was doing what monks do: praying.

Admittedly, I was a monk too, albeit a reluctant one, but at least they had not yet cut my hair — something of a glory in my case — into that ridiculous roundel that the rest of them wore. I had claimed a dreadful case of ringworm the day I was due to be tonsured and thus saved my hair. And that meant that I did not *look* like a monk, apart from my clothes.

"Here, help me," I whispered to Brother Odo, as I reached for the dead Dane.

"What are you doing?" he asked.

"Stripping him."

The monk stared at me. Then a look of understanding came over his face. "You think he will have treasure hidden on him? Gold, silver, jewels."

"I don't care if he has all the treasure of the Caliph hidden in his belt. What I want is his clothes." I was struggling to get the man's tunic off over his head. "Grab that end."

Brother Odo obediently grasped one side of the tunic and together we managed to peel it over the man's head. He was wearing a padded undershirt. I prodded it. The thing was seething with lice.

"Maybe not that."

Brother Odo reached, questioningly, for the man's cloak and I nodded, while struggling to hitch my own filthy habit up over my head.

"I know your clothes are dirty," Brother Odo whispered as I struggled to take the habit off, "but wouldn't it be better to wait until later to change?"

Reaching for the Dane's tunic, I shook my head. "I have an idea. Get his shoes."

While I pulled the Dane's tunic over my shoulders — it was still warm from him — Brother Odo untied the man's shoes. I thought about asking for the trousers too, but having seen how lousy his undershirt was, I thought better of it.

With the man's tunic on, I fastened his cloak around my shoulders, but I turned it so that it hung open at the front rather than over my right arm. The Northmen wear their cloaks offset so that their sword arm is free, whereas we wear ours centrally. It's warmer that way, but it makes trying to draw a sword quickly more difficult. But my aim was not to pretend to be a Dane, rather to make it clear that I was not a monk.

"How do I look?"

"How are you supposed to look?" Brother Odo asked.

"Never mind." But as I shook my head a spasm gripped my bowels, threatening to loose their contents into my breeches.

Brother Odo's expression turned to one of concern. "Are you all right?"

"It's nothing," I gasped, my bowels still griping. "Old — old wound."

The old wound of fear. In my head, voices were clamouring, telling me to stay down, stay hidden, stay safe. Anything but walk out among the Danes.

"Do you trust me, Brother Odo?"

Brother Odo looked at me with all the wide-eyed trust of a new born sucking on his mother's teat.

"Of course I do, Brother Conrad."

"Because for this to work you must trust me absolutely."

"I do, Brother Conrad, I do."

"Good. Now, stay here. And whatever you see or hear, remember, it's all part of the plan. You understand?"

"All part of the plan," said Brother Odo.

"Right." I said.

"Right," said Brother Odo, encouragingly.

"Right," I repeated, unable to bring myself to leave the cover of the sty.

"Right?" said Brother Odo.

"Right…" I said and rolled out of the sty.

"Part of the plan," I whispered as I saw Brother Odo's questioning face, then I put myself to crawling towards the not-so-distant yet impossibly far away bank that marked the edge of the monastery enclosure.

In truth, there were three plans.

Plan number one was to crawl to the bank and get as far away as possible before anyone saw me.

"Oi!"

Plan number two.

I stood up and waved towards the lookout. Now, so long as he didn't have the sight of a hawk, he'd just see another Dane, unsteady on his legs from drinking victory.

Unfortunately, he *did* have the sight of a hawk.

The Dane jumped down from the bank and started making his way towards me.

Plan number three.

"Hey, Erik," I yelled to him — if you don't know the name of a Dane, just call him Erik, they all answer to it — "Get over here, I've found something for you."

The Dane jogged over, his spear held lightly but at the ready. He stopped at the edge of spear range.

I held my hand up in greeting but he made no move to answer in kind.

"You speak our tongue," he said, "but you're no Dane. Are you one of Torvik's lads?"

For a moment I thought of making this plan four. But I had no way of knowing if there really was a Torvik; he could have been testing me.

I shook my head.

"Trader," I said. "Slave trader. The moment I heard you were harvesting Medeshamstede Abbey, I followed." I tapped my nose. "Ivarr uses me

19

to sell on all the slaves he takes — saves him having to herd them off to Dubhlinn."

But Erik, assuming his name *was* Erik, wasn't so easily convinced.

"Where are your men then?" he asked. "You cannot take slaves to market on your own."

"No, no, no," I said. I smiled, my broad, I'm-taking-you-into-my-confidence smile. "Do you think I would bring all the boats and men and chains and irons with me when I don't even know what the goods are like? Not that they are far mind, just downriver on the Nene where it joins the Wash — you must have passed our camp when you sailed upriver. Near the saltings at Lun? You saw us?"

Erik shook his head. "No."

"No, of course not, stupid of me. Dark night, no moon, you're hardly going to see us, are you? But I saw you. I find it hard to sleep sometimes, and I looked out and saw you, heading upriver and I thought to myself, now where can they be going, up the Nene? Then I knew: Medeshamstede! So I got my skiff, told my men to wait, and set off after you to see what the catch was like. Now, where's your earl? I'd better speak to him about selling on his take."

Erik — I still didn't know his name, but he certainly looked like an Erik — shook his head.

"How do I know you're what you say you are?"

"How do you know?" I turned round. "Because I'm going to add to your takings for the day." I pointed at the sty. "In there."

Erik was experienced enough not to walk alone into a structure at the word of a stranger — which is what I'd been counting on, given that there was a dead Dane inside the sty.

"You do it," he said.

"Happy to."

Marching up to the sty I stood outside and whistled.

"Out," I said. "We know you're in there; don't make us come and get you."

I waited. Nothing. Damn it, Brother Odo was taking literally my orders to stay put. I glanced round at Erik the Dane, putting on a show of exasperation for him.

"Come out, come out," I said. "We know you're in there." Then, lower, so Erik couldn't hear, I whispered, "It's all right, Brother Odo, come out."

Still nothing.

Finally, I leaned down and peered into the sty. There, hunched up against its far wall, I could see Brother Odo. If his face hadn't been covered with mud and manure, I suspect it would have been white with fear. I glanced back. Erik the Dane was still just about far enough back for me to risk a whisper.

"It's part of the plan."

I beckoned Brother Odo to me.

And, for a wonder, he came. Unsteady and unsure, but he came, crawling out of the opening and blinking uncertainly at Erik.

The Dane laughed.

"Ha, another one of these soft god toys. They are fit for nothing and sell for less."

"At the markets *you* take them to," I said. "Give them to me, and I will bring back enough gold to sink your boat."

"Come to the earl," said Erik. "He will decide." The Dane jabbed the spear at Brother Odo. "Go," he said. But, of course, he spoke in the language of the Danes, and so Brother Odo looked blankly at him. However, a second jab of the spear conveyed the meaning and Brother Odo started stumbling towards the monastery church and the slowly growing pile of loot lying at the feet of the earl of the Northmen.

Erik made the courtesy to his earl, then pointed to me.

"This one says he is a trader in slaves, come to see what we have to sell." He pointed at the slight and shivering figure of Brother Odo. "He found this one, hiding in the pig sty, and brought him out to me."

The earl looked at me. I looked at him. Or rather, I looked up at him. A long way up.

"My, you really are tall," I said. "Earl Thorgrim?"

The earl looked down at me, his eyes narrowing as he sought, in the way of the Northmen, to see through my eyes to my soul. They place great store in their ability to tell a man's worth and his truth from how he meets this appraising gaze.

I looked steadily back, fixing my gaze on the middle of his forehead. For I have learned a trick: look there, and to the man searching for your soul it will seem that you are responding with open eyes and open heart, when all the time your soul is hidden in the misdirection of your eyes.

"Thorgrim the Tall," the earl said. "For the obvious reason."

"I am Conrad, trader in slaves and silver, in gold and garnets, in all the wealth of the east and the treasure of the Romans." I made the courtesy as elaborately as I might, then looked up to Thorgrim the Tall once more. "I am here to make you rich."

The earl laughed. It was a surprisingly high-pitched sound.

"I am already rich," he said.

"I will make you richer," I said. "So rich that you will look upon your ships, heavy laden with treasure, and wonder if they will bear you back home, so low do they ride in the water."

"But I am not going home," said Thorgrim. "My home shall be in this land, that I have taken for myself."

"Even better," I said, "for then your boats will not founder and the gold I will earn for you will not go into the deeps but shall be gathered to your hearth and given to your men. And how many men there will be! Gathering at the gold call, heeding its song and sailing their long boats over the grey road to the hall of the ring giver, Thorgrim the Tall."

"How will you get me this gold?"

I pointed at the meagre pile of spoils laying at his feet.

"It won't be too difficult — what you have here is bare enough to satisfy a warrior still growing his first beard."

"I heard this was a rich house. So far, it has not proved to be."

I smiled, and this time I looked into his eyes and saw that his soul was enflamed with the gold lust.

"It is. You simply need to know where to look."

"Where should I look?"

"Where I will show you."

Earl Thorgrim held out his hand, indicating that I should lead.

I made the courtesy then pointed at Brother Odo. "I shall need to bring him."

Thorgrim nodded.

With the earl, and five of his household men, following, I took Brother Odo by the arm and led him towards the bank on the further side of the compound, towards the thick stands of gorse and thorn that clustered at the base of the bank.

"This is all part of the plan," I whispered to him as we went, and I saw his eyes widening as he slowly began to suspect what I planned to do.

"You can't," he whispered back.

"This way, they will live, and we can free them."

"Better the red crown," said Brother Odo.

"You said you trusted me. Trust me now."

Brother Odo cast an agonised glance in my direction. I gave him my most trustworthy look.

"It's part of the plan?"

"Completely."

Brother Odo looked as if he was being torn in two.

I stopped and grasped his arm.

"Trust me," I said. Brother Odo, seeing my open and honest gaze, slowly nodded.

"Yes," he whispered.

"Then go in and bring them out," I said. "It would be better than the Danes doing it."

He nodded.

I let him go. "Go on."

As Brother Odo turned and disappeared in among the gorse bushes, Earl Thorgrim stepped forward but I held up my hand. "It's all right. He will bring out the treasure that you have been unable to find." I smiled. "Human treasure. The best kind of treasure for a slave trader."

But you do not stay earl of the Northmen for long by trusting to the words of another. Thorgrim signalled his men forward to cover each side of the tunnel, while his warmaster whistled others to them.

I stood near the earl, affecting an attitude of easy nonchalance, as if I knew without doubt that Brother Odo would soon re-emerge with many others in his wake, ready to give themselves into the keeping of the Northmen. But as the wait lengthened, and I felt eyes being cast upon me, cold fear fingers clutched my bowels. Thorgrim, seeing my gripe, asked me on it.

"No, no," I answered. "It is nothing. An old wound. It sometimes plagues me, particularly when I am near water."

Water. Even as I spoke, the fear grew. Perhaps there was a tunnel from the hiding place to the river. The Nene was thickly lined with willow and alder. There were many places where small boats might be concealed. Mayhap Brother Odo had found his brethren gone and followed them.

I could not stop my eyes from wandering to the hard gazes being turned upon me. These were eyes that measured lives in weights of silver and gold; my own was being weighed as I stood and waited.

Even as I began to despair there came a movement and rustle through the thorns. The men guarding tensed, drawing sword or hoisting spear. Earl Thorgrim's gaze flicked to me and then back to the thorn grove.

Brother Odo was first to emerge. He came out, his face white and streaked as if with tears, but after him came the others. One by one, they emerged: a full two thirds of the monks of the abbey, and a quarter of the abbey's servants. They came out, blinking and helpless as babies dropped from their mothers' wombs, and the Danes took them and bound them as they came, swaddling them in ropes and chains.

Last of all was the abbot, Flory. He came out and, emerging, turned as if searching for me. But before he could find me one of the Danes kicked his knees out from under him. On the ground, they bound him like a piglet bound for market and, when he began to speak, they stuffed a rag into his mouth.

A bit of a relief really. One thing I'd learned during my time in the monastery was that when the abbot began to speak it was impossible to stop him.

As the monks and servants were herded off towards the pens set aside for them, Brother Odo ran towards me. Before any of the Danes could catch him — he was thin and fleet — he reached me, stumbling on to his knees at my feet.

He looked up at me with all the forlorn hope of a woman wishing to reclaim her virginity.

"It's all part of the plan?"

I glanced past him and saw his pursuers — a pair of angry-looking Danes — fast approaching.

Hope is what gives people reason to rise from their sleep and face another day of toil.

"Yes," I said, just as the club of the leading Dane swung into the back of Brother Odo's skull and sent him into the embrace of sleep.

Hope, that pitiless taskmaster, might drag other people from their beds but gold was what woke me up in the morning.

I turned to Earl Thorgrim.

"There is a winter market in the week after St Andrew's day; I know the traders who come there. Send the men you have taken with me and I will earn you more silver than you will make on them in Dubhlinn, where all the merchants are villains and thieves. Besides, it is many weeks before the next market by the banks of the black pool, and you will have to feed them until then."

"I don't have to feed them," said Earl Thorgrim.

"No, you don't," I agreed. "But then they will fetch less when the time comes to sell them. Give them over to me to sell and they will come to market well fed, fit and strong. The slave traders will pay good silver, gold too, for such a haul."

"And you would return with this silver once you have sold them for me?"

"Of course. All know that those who betray Thorgrim the Tall do not live long to tell the tale. Besides, I would not say give so many men into my keeping alone. No, send them with an escort of your own men, that they — and I — might be guarded." I paused. The earl was thinking on it. "Furthermore, it would save you attending the market yourself, and a slave market is no great joy even to those selling. Only the silver and gold make it worthwhile."

Thorgrim the Tall nodded slowly.

"That is true," he said. "Although enough silver and gold will make even the grimmest market sweeter in the memory."

"Then how much sweeter will this market be when all you have is the silver and gold, and no memory of the cries of women and children, and the pleading of men?"

Thorgrim looked down upon me. "If you play me false, Conrad, I will hunt you and I will kill you."

"Slowly, no doubt."

"Very slowly."

"Tell me, what is the longest you have drawn out the killing of a man?"

"There was a man, a Saxon, who said he would bring me to the abbey of the East Angles that lies in the midst of the fens and meres of their country, and that is said to be the richest of all the abbeys in their land. I should have known better than to trust the word of a Saxon about the whereabouts of a monastery of the Angles, but by the time I realised he had no more idea of the way through the marshes than I did, we had spent three days wading through mud and marsh. In recompense, it took him as long to die."

"That is impressive indeed," I said. "But I have heard tell that the Caliph in the east may keep a man begging for death for a year before granting his request."

The earl sniffed. "I have been to those far lands, where the sun is hot and the skin of men dark, and I say to you that they are not so wise and subtle as they believe. For they believe in one god to whom they are slaves, but we have many gods and we are beholden to none, but follow each as we like, as free men."

"But the men of this island, they follow one god, and they say they are his sons. Is that not best of all?"

The Dane looked at me carefully. "Are you not one of the men of this island?"

"I am," I said. "But it seems best to me to call upon whichever god is closest, and best of all to trust to fortune, for she has ever favoured me."

"Fortune!" The earl shook his head, but there was a smile upon his face. "Ha, she may raise a man higher than the highest god, then cast him down again." He looked at me closely. "I would not dare plight myself to this mistress. It is a brave or foolhardy man who does so. Since you seem no fool, then I must think you brave."

There are times when it is better to say nothing.

Earl Thorgrim nodded. "Very well. I will give you these men and women we have taken, with a suitable guard, that you may sell them for me. But what do you ask in return? For a man such as you would not do such things without hope of gain."

I affected a laugh as untroubled as the dawn.

"Men speak truly when they say Earl Thorgrim sees as far as he stands above other men. You ask want I ask in return? As token of the great liberality for which you are known throughout these lands and beyond the grey sea, I ask that you give me the smallest part of my hand for each of these I sell." I held up my right hand, fingers spread, then bent fingers and thumb until only the smallest finger remained.

"One fifth?" Earl Thorgrim shook his head, then held up both hands, fingers splayed, before closing all the fingers save only the little finger on his left hand. "One tenth. And be thankful it is cold, lest I remove my boots and bring my toes into this reckoning."

"My lord is generous," I said.

"I am." Thorgrim gestured one of his men closer. "You will lead the guard that will take this man and the slaves to market. Watch him well. If he seeks to play you false, or to escape, cut off his feet and bring him back to me."

The Dane, as broad and muscled as Thorgrim was tall and lean, turned eyes that were as grey and bleak as the sea in winter upon me.

"Yes," he said. "I will."

"Thank you, lord," I said to the earl. "With such a guard, I will surely be safe taking even so valuable a cargo to market." I turned to the guard. "As we are to be companions upon the road, it would be good for me to know your name."

"Erik," he said.

"Of course."

Chapter 2

There is a skill to getting the best price when selling people as slaves, and I have that skill. As the penalty for failing to get the best price for the men and women Thorgrim's warriors had taken at Medeshamstede would be a long and painful death, I employed all my skill in the sale of the monks and servants of the abbey — a sale that lived long in the memory of the people who attended it and even longer in the minds of those sold during it.

It was a beach market. There were ships hauled up on the strand belonging to traders from all the kingdoms of these islands, be they Angle or Saxon, Pict or Scot, Briton or Gael, not to mention far traders from the lands of the Northmen, Franks from across the Narrow Sea, Belgi and Alemanni, Frisians and Wends, as well as agents of the Emperor and even traders whose dark skin and thick-huddled robes told the tale of their arrival from the kingdom of the Caliph. Despite the season, they had come to buy because these islands are known for selling the best slaves and hunting dogs east of the ocean and under the sun. Admittedly, the dogs usually sold for more than the people — if I had had a pack of hounds I could have bought the monks of three abbeys and still had enough change for a couple of priests and a deacon. But I had twenty-three monks, eleven servants and eight women (with associated babes that were usually thrown in free of charge, on the basis that they would be able to do some useful work once they'd grown up and letting them go with their mothers ensured that the women wouldn't mope too much). Counting them up as Erik had marched them on to the boats to sail them downstream to the market, I concluded that the monastery's servants were either fleeter of foot or smarter of wit than the monks: before rumour of the Northmen had reached the abbey, it must have been home to at least fifty servants, not to mention their families. Most of them had, evidently, decided to leave before the Danes arrived. The monks had mainly stayed, although twenty-three was still fewer than I had expected: either a larger party than Brother Odo thought had taken the Gospel Book to the kingdom of the East Angles or nearly a third of the fraternity had decided to flee rather than hide.

The skill in selling slaves lies in the order of sale. The market itself was due to last for the week after Christmas, but I knew well that most of the money would be spent in the first three days, with a splurge on the last day as traders made final offers before making their way home again. We had arrived in time for the start of the market, but asking around I learned that some traders, delayed by adverse wind and weather, had not yet arrived. So, I put my wares on display, ensuring that a reluctant Erik had his men put up wind breaks and rough shelters for the soon-to-be slaves, while I looked at what else was on offer.

Not much, was the answer. One or two pinched families selling themselves into slavery for the hope of food, and a handful of even more wretched outlaws. Next to these meagre gleanings, my display of well-fed monks stood out as starkly as a garnet dropped on a dung heap.

Erik protested again when I told him that we must feed the monks well while we waited for the sale — he seemed to think it was all a matter of turning up, selling and then sailing back to Thorgrim.

"No, no," I told him. "We're here to bring your lord back so much gold he'll worry about his ship foundering." I looked the squat Dane in the eye — being short among his kind, I could do that — and added, "The more we get, the more your generous lord will give you, I should think."

So Erik had kept the monks and the rest of them fed and, relatively, warm and dry, while I walked the market, striking up conversations with the other traders, rekindling some old acquaintances, and letting on to one or two, those least able to keep a story quiet, that I was here as agent to sell these monks, not as the vendor, and that I would be bidding myself.

So when the final day of the market dawned, and with it came the last of the traders, running before the dawn wind to catch the market's closing bargains, I knew that there was a great wash of silver and gold waiting to be spent upon the human harvest I had brought to sale.

In such circumstances, it was best to begin with a taste of what was available, to whet the greed of the buyers.

"What am I bid for this lovely family: Blecca a master carter, his wife Siflæd who is a sound seamstress and their son, Wada, who will at least serve a shift pulling his father's cart?"

I may have been stretching the description: I had seen Blecca beat his wife until she bled, only for Siflæd to break an ox bone over Blecca's head, while their son was so addle-pated that even an ox seemed quick in comparison.

I looked around at the sea of faces: curious, veiled, greedy, cautious. All the stripes of merchant, and each fingering his purse and calculating gain and cost while looking round to see who would be first to speak.

Well, that would be me then.

"If none of you niggards will bid, *I* will." I pointed at the family, then held up my other hand with three shiny silver pennies blinking in the wintry light between my fingers. "I thank you for making such a present to me... "

"Wait." From the middle of the group of merchants, a man, a Frank by the sound of him, held up his hand. "Four pennies."

"Five."

"Six."

I could hardly keep up. That first family went for twelve silver pennies — a good price for such bargain level people — and, looking out upon the crowd, I could see their appetite for spending money, real, proper money, had been whetted. As the carter, his wife and idiot son were led off, I signalled Erik to bring me the next lot for sale.

The real money was waiting for the monks, but those merchants, with their sharp eyes and sharper fingers, would wait. First, I would sell off the dross to the visiting thane or local cottager, breathless with the excitement of the sale and with not the wit to realise what they were buying. So it was relatively quick work to dispose of the servants, slaves and peasants that I had brought from the abbey. The women, unfortunately, were none of them pleasing to the eye, so the best I could hope for was selling them to the wife of some churl to help with the chores. They came and went quietly enough: to have survived the raid by the Danes was more than they had hoped and to be sold to their own people was a better fate than they feared.

But on the journey downriver to the market, I had whispered word to Brother Odo, to pass on to his fellow monks, that this was all part of my plan. Yes, it might seem that I was selling them off to slave traders from the farthest flung parts of the world, but it was a ruse: I was, I let Brother Odo know, buying them all for myself, through agents, to give them back their freedom and their abbey once the Danes had gone.

All nonsense, of course, but it ensured we didn't have any trouble from the monks. Indeed, Erik had even pulled me aside, while we waited at market for the richer traders to arrive, to ask if I had put some wit-dulling potion in the monks' ale, so docile did he find them. Naturally, I told him yes, alluding to knowledge gained from a mother who was of the cunning folk, and enjoying the wary look with which he greeted my hint at knowledge of things ungrasped and unseen. Erik would be careful when he shared plates with me from now on, and as we spoke I saw his hand twist into the sign against the elf eye.

So now it was time to sell the monks. This was what I had been leading up to. This gave the far traders reason to open their purses and take out their gold. For these monks were educated: almost all could read and most could write. They made ideal slaves for the lord of some distant fief to parade before his ignorant neighbours, as well as providing a scribe to write and read charters and letters.

As the first of the monks was brought forward for sale, I saw those merchants who had come far and who had the biggest purses slide forward through the crowd.

"Here we have the first of our star items for sale today: a monk, late of the abbey at Medeshamstede, well fed, healthy and, more to the point, able to read and write."

"How do we know he can read and write?" voice yelled from the crowd.

I searched for the speaker, and saw him.

"Master Fulk, always a pleasure to hear from you. I should think the fact that I am bidding three shillings — yes, Master Fulk, three whole shillings — for this monk should convince you." And I held up the shillings for all to see. All earned earlier in the sale, but none there realised that I was buying with their money.

It was straightforward after that. I spoke quietly to each monk as he was sold, reassuring them that I would soon reclaim them, that it was all part of the plan. I did wonder, in passing, quite when they would realise that the plan was actually to make me a lot of money: when they were embarked upon their ships, when they were sailing across the whale road, when they were bundled off their ships and taken to their new homes? Some, I thought, would still be looking for me to appear upon the horizon with their manumission after years of slavery.

Hope is what keeps fools going.

I saved Abbot Flory for second to last. The abbot blinked warily at the crowd staring up at him. Standing next to Erik, he appeared lean, like a sapling shrivelled by winter winds. He blinked at me, as if trying to remember who I was, and I wondered if there was more truth in what I had told the Dane than I knew, for the abbot's wits appeared to have been lost to him. But I have seen this happen to men of power: when their authority is stripped from them, they shrivel in the eyes of the world, like husks of hollowed-out corn.

"Now here," I announced to the crowd, "I offer a truly exceptional item for sale. It is rare indeed for a man such as this to be offered at market. A man of power and standing, a man of high birth and high learning. The erstwhile abbot of the great monastery at Medeshamstede is now available to any one of you with sufficient funds. Just think of the possibilities should you acquire this man: the connections he can forge for you, the ransom you can demand for him to be redeemed, maybe…" and here I dropped my voice to bring the crowd in closer to me, "maybe even the whereabouts of the monastery's hidden treasures, for I tell you truly, the Danes found only a small part of it." Standing tall once more, and speaking loudly, I asked, "What am I bid for the

Abbot Flory?"

I'd barely got the words out before the first bid came in. A few frantic minutes later, I had sold Abbot Flory for two pounds and six shillings. Even the abbot appeared flattered by the sum he had commanded — or at least he was, until he saw who had bought him.

No Nose Fergus had, as his name suggested, mislaid his nose in a fight some years before. Where his nose had been, dull red scar tissue now hissed in and out with each breath, making him look like a respiring side of hanging beef. But the truly frightening things about Fergus were his eyes: one was washed-out blue, the other dull grey, and each with the life of a week-dead trout. When Abbot Flory realised who had bought him he turned his own, suddenly panic-stricken, eyes towards me and grasped my arm.

"It's true? It's all part of the plan?" he hissed.

No Nose Fergus's men grabbed the abbot and dragged him away, but as he was pulled backwards I could see him pleading for reassurance.

Call me soft, but I mouthed back at him, "It's all part of the plan," and, seeing the words, I saw him relax and nod.

Always leave them with enough hope to live another day, that's what I say.

Speaking of hope, I turned to Brother Odo. I'd left him to last in the hope that somebody would decide to spend a few pennies on the market's gleanings but seeing him, scrawny and crook legged, standing on the platform, while the traders, satisfied with their buys, were already beginning to head back to their ships and their wagons, I began to worry.

"Wait up, wait up!" I yelled, trying to stop the exodus, "I saved the best for last."

The laugh that greeted my pitch indicated that I might have made a mistake.

"Go on, then, Conrad, if you think he's so great, you bid for him."

I looked to see who had made that suggestion and saw Rolf the Fat smiling up at me through the layers of blubber that rolled under his chin and above his tunic. Of course, he'd be one of the last to leave: his men were busy herding the slaves he'd bought onto his ship and then they'd come back to load the merchant onto his chair and carry him aboard.

"He's better than he looks," I said. "Educated, literate, good with children," — Brother Odo brightened at the suggestion — "he'd make the ideal slave and teacher for the son of a thane wanting to equip his son for our new world of charters and documents."

"You bid for him then," said Rolf, his little piggy eyes dancing with glee.

He knew he had me. *I* knew he had me.

"Five pennies," I said, weakly.

Rolf the Fat laughed, a big, rolling, booming laugh.

"Four pennies," he bid.

"Three pennies," shouted Pepin the Hairy.

"Two pennies," bid Honest Gunther (he wasn't).

"One penny," cried Rolf the Fat, and he really was crying now, fat tears rolling down his fat cheeks as his belly wobbled uncontrollably with laughter.

I looked round the crowd, looking for bids and, seeing none, shouted out, "He's going, he's going, he's…gone!"

Brother Odo looked at me, trying to understand what had just happened.

"Who's bought me?" he asked, staring round wildly.

"Why, I have," I said. I smiled at him. "You're all mine."

Brother Odo looked askance at me. "That's… that's good, isn't it? It's all part of the plan?"

"Oh, yes," I said, "it's all part of the plan."

Chapter 3

"Shouldn't we be following the abbot?"

Brother Odo looked up at me. He was trudging along the track, his feet occasionally disappearing up to the shanks in the mud. Then he would stop, grab hold of his knee with his hands, and haul the foot from the sucking mud.

I looked down at him from my seat astride a small but sturdy pony. The pony, an intelligent beast, seemed to know where to find the harder ground beneath the muddy track: its hooves had only stuck once or twice so far on our ride.

"We are," I said.

"But, but I saw that man with the ugly face take him aboard his ship to the country of the Gaels." Brother Odo's foot sank, with a sucking glop, into another mud pit, and stuck fast. "We are standing on a muddy track in the land of the East Angles."

"Exactly," I said, and urged the pony on. Brother Odo tried to follow; the loud, squelching splat I heard shortly afterwards told me that the mud hole had refused to release its hold.

I reined the pony to a halt before looking round.

"Not again," I said.

Brother Odo lifted his face from where it had splashed into the mud. "Sorry," he said.

Sighing, I turned the pony round and rode back to Brother Odo, stopping next to him so that the monk could use the animal's sturdy leg as a hand hold to help himself up.

"Make sure you brush that mud off him," I said, pointing to the hand prints on the pony's leg and flank. "He cost me two shillings."

As Brother Odo made an ineffectual attempt to clean the mud from my pony, I heard him muttering under his breath. I've learned many things over the years, and one of them is never let a slave get away with muttering against you in your presence; it only gives them ideas.

"What were you saying?"

Brother Odo looked up at me, startled.

"Pardon?"

"What were you muttering about? I heard you."

Even through the thick layer of mud covering his cheeks, I could see the monk blush. He mumbled something about Bede.

"I know Bede," I said. "It'll go better for you if you tell me what you were saying, for my ears are sharp and my eyes keen."

Brother Odo paused, then launched into his account. "Blessed Bishop Aidan, when he was given a horse by King Oswine, gave the horse away to a poor man, only for the king to tell him off for giving his present away. But then Bishop Aidan said to the king, 'Are you telling me that this son of Adam is less valuable to you than the son of a mare you gave me?' And the king went down upon his knees before Bishop Aidan and begged his forgiveness." Brother Odo looked up at me, blushing even more furiously.

Naturally, I buffeted him round the ear.

"You are definitely not worth more than this pony," I said. "No one was willing to pay anything for you, whereas this pony cost me two shillings."

Brother Odo nodded, crestfallen. While slavery is a fate few desire, even fewer want to be found so inadequate that no one wants them, even as a slave.

"As to what we're doing here in the land of the East Angles," I leaned down to Brother Odo and patted him on the cheek, "you're part of the plan."

"Me?" said Brother Odo, brightening suddenly. "I'm part of the plan?"

"Absolutely," I said. "Come on, I'll tell you as we go. Just try not to fall over again."

So as we made our way along the muddy track towards the royal estate at *Beodricesworth* I explained the plan — well, the parts of it I wanted Brother Odo to know.

"By selling your brothers…"

"*Our* brothers," said Brother Odo.

"Our brothers," I agreed, "I saved their lives. What's more, I got a very good price for them, so much so that even the gold grubbing eyes of Earl Thorgrim widened when I laid the money before him. He was so grateful he even gave me most of what he had promised. But it is not enough to manumit our brothers. For that, we shall need something else, something truly precious and wonderful." I looked down at Brother Odo, trotting beside me, his eyes wide with the tell-me-what-happens-next wonder of a boy listening to the stories of an old warrior.

"The Book."

"The book?"

"*The* Book," I said.

"Ah, yes, the Book," said Brother Odo. "That is why we are going to the kingdom of the East Angles. Of course." He looked the question at me. "You would not sell the Book?"

"Me? Sell the Book? Sell *The* Book? How can you ask such a thing?"

"I — I am sorry," said Brother Odo. "But then, how will you remit our brothers?"

"With the Book," I said. "What else?"

And Brother Odo's eyes widened as his faith overflowed into wonder. "Yes, yes." He looked at me, his eyes as bright with that faith as the winter sun on flat water, and said, "We will take the Book of Life and raise it high, as Moses raised the bronze serpent in the desert, and all our brethren and those who have taken them into slavery will be called to life."

"Exactly," I said. "But first we must find the Book, and then we must take it. Which is why I have brought you with me, Brother Odo."

"Me?"

"I doubt that brothers Gadd, Chad and Ræd would accept my word for it when I arrive at the hall of King Edmund and say that I've come to take the Book from their keeping. After all, I am relatively new to the community, and they know me but a little, although I like to think I have managed to gain a name for honesty and straight dealing. But you, Brother Odo, everyone knows, and everyone trusts. If you say we are to take the Book, then they will believe you." I leaned down closer to the monk and whispered. "But, to be certain, I would tell them that we come under the authority of Abbot Flory to take the Book into our keeping."

Brother Odo looked troubled. "I am sure he would want us to do so, Brother Conrad, but he did not give me such a command. It would be an untruth to tell Brother Gadd, Brother Chad and Brother Ræd otherwise."

"Ah," I tapped my nose, "it is all part of the plan — and you know that Abbot Flory agreed to the plan."

"Oh, oh yes." Brother Odo nodded. "I see now." He slammed the heel of his hand against his forehead. "I am so dull of wit, Brother Conrad. A man of subtlety like you must despair of one so slow as I."

"Nonsense, nonsense," I laughed, and clouted him round the head, before pointing ahead. "Dull of wit you may be, but sharp of eye. What see you ahead?"

Brother Odo shaded his eyes against the slanting winter sunlight.

"It is a great hall, roofed gold it seems at this hour, with a great press of houses and huts gathered round it as piglets round a sow."

"It is *Beodricesworth*. We have arrived."

"Oh, good," said Brother Odo. Then, inexplicably, he blushed, and struck himself across the cheek.

I had spent many hours in the saddle and I was tired. *Beodricesworth* lay within an hour's ride. I could have just ignored Brother Odo's actions as yet another instance of his oddity. But curiosity has always been my besetting sin. Well, no it hasn't; cupidity, concupiscence and cowardice have warmer places in my heart, but I preferred to have a quaternary of errors rather than a trinity of faults, so on this occasion I added curiosity to the list — and saved my life. Although I didn't know it yet.

"All right," I said. "You've exceeded my expectations: you've surprised me. So, tell me why you blushed and then slapped yourself."

Brother Odo blushed again. "You noticed?"

"I could warm my hands from the heat of your blush, Brother Odo."

"I am sorry, I did not mean to disturb you," said Brother Odo. "But I blushed for realising the deep selfishness of my heart."

"In what way?"

"When you told me the town we see ahead is *Beodricesworth* I rejoiced, for I realised that we should be able to find a warm place by the fire."

"What is wrong or selfish about that?" I asked. The wind had been bitter through most of our journey and although it had died away, my feet and fingers were still numb from it.

"I was glad because *Beodricesworth* is close."

"After a journey like today's, anyone would be."

"But if it had been further away, then the people following us would have got there first and they would have taken all the warm places by the fire." Brother Odo looked up at me, his face scarlet with shame. "That is when I realised the deep selfishness of my heart, for I would rather take the warm place by the fire myself than give it up to another."

"Wait a moment," I said. "What people following us?"

"Those people," said Brother Odo, pointing back the way we'd come.

I turned in the saddle and saw, to my slowly mounting horror, a group of horsemen, spear tips silver glitter in the westering sun, riding after us. Even at this distance, I could see that there were more than twenty and, from the way the forest of raised spears swayed like wind grass, I suspected that the column stretched many, many yards back along the way.

"Ride!" I yelled, jabbing my heels as hard as I could into the pony's flanks.

The beast, exhausted at the end of a day trudging through mud, barely even raised its head, but continued plodding along at exactly the same pace as before.

Brother Odo patted the beast's neck and looked up at me.

"Don't worry. They are still far behind. I think we will get to the king's hall first and have our choice of the warm places by the fire." I looked down at the monk, now offering some words of encouragement to my beast. It was probably just as well he was looking at the horse, or he would have seen me gibbering with fear.

"D — Danes," I stuttered.

"What?" said Brother Odo.

"They — they're Danes," I repeated.

Brother Odo looked up at me, wide eyed and then, without a single word or glance, he was off, running pell-mell down the track towards *Beodricesworth*, his habit hitched up to his knees.

"Wait!" I yelled, "wait, God damn it!" while I kicked my pony's flanks to no effect.

At my shout, Brother Odo stopped, cast an agonised glance over his shoulder, then came running back to me.

"The beast is blown," I said, getting down from the pony as Brother Odo reached me. "You'll have to carry me."

Before Brother Odo could say anything, I'd jumped on his back. His arms had risen to take hold of my legs without thought — a sure indication of many games played with the children of the monastery when Abbot Flory wasn't watching — and I kicked his flanks with all the vigour of a man trying to escape an oncoming column of Danes.

Obedient to the command, Brother Odo began trotting towards *Beodricesworth*. Another kick took him to a canter, and a third had him galloping.

But before we had gone more than fifty yards I heard the thump of closing hoof beats.

I looked round, feeling the fear gorge rise up my throat as my back tickled at the prospect of a spear head being plunged into it, and saw my pony galloping up after us. Apparently, seeing its friend Brother Odo galloping away, it had gathered its remaining strength and followed.

For a moment I thought of transferring back to the pony. But Brother Odo was fresher. I stayed on him.

So, riding before the storm, we arrived at the hall of Edmund, King

45

of the East Angles.

Chapter 4

"I have word for the king."

The door warden barely glanced at us when we arrived at the entrance to the king's great hall. He was staring beyond us to where the column of riders was slowly resolving into a mass of armed men at least thirty strong. At the sight, his face resolved into an expression of horror.

Brother Odo was standing with his hands on his knees while his lungs pumped like a blacksmith's bellows. The pony, standing next to him, had adopted a similar position.

"Danes," the door warden whispered, looking at me with terror-struck eyes.

"Yes," I said. "Let me through." I pointed at Brother Odo. "Him too, when he can move."

The door warden pushed open the doors to the king's hall. Inside, all was tumult. Men were running to fetch swords and shields and armour from where they hung, the slaves were clearing the tables and rushing to store plates and spoons and wine, while the women of the king's household had gathered in determined silence round the queen, who stood near the great fire with needles and thread and frames about her, for she had been engaged in stringing a tapestry upon her loom when the news broke upon the court of the East Angles.

Of the king, I could see no sign.

More importantly, I could not see the three monks whom Abbot Flory had sent from Medeshamstede with the Book. Surely we had not come this far, riding before the oncoming Danes, only to find out that the monks had absconded with the Book themselves.

I grabbed hold of a passing slave, shaking him from the panic that was sending him scuttling around without any apparent purpose.

"Three monks from Medeshamstede Abbey. Have they arrived?"

The slave looked at me, his eyes clearing a little as he was asked something that he could actually answer.

"Yes, they arrived two weeks past. They are in the church. The king is with them."

Two answers for one question. Sometimes I almost think fortune favours me too highly — and then I think again.

Making my way out of the hall, I had to dodge men, women and children running hither and thither, few of whom seemed to be accomplishing anything of note. The place looked like the ants' nest I had poured boiling water into when I was a child — only the ants had reasserted order more quickly.

Emerging from the confusion, I saw that at least some of the king's household warriors were forming a line before the king's hall. *Beodricesworth* was no sort of stronghold; there was a hall to milk the rich lands that lay round about, with a huge thorn stockade to hold the tribute sheep, goats and cattle, and barns near as big as the king's hall to store the rendered grain and oats and wheat, not to mention sheds that were loaded with stored apples and pears and other dried fruit. The only defence of the king's hall lay in the swords and spears of the king's men, and they were marshalling in front of the hall.

They weren't a fearsome bunch: a mixture of grizzled old retainers, better suited to huddling for warmth by the fire and telling stories of the deeds they had once done, and youths barely old enough to grow a fuzz on their cheeks. I looked to the hall, thinking perhaps the king's best men were still inside, putting on armour and helmet, but the door shutting, and the sound of it being barred, told me the truth of that hope. This was all there was.

"Come on," I said, grabbing the scruff of Brother Odo's neck and hauling him upright, "I need you."

Coughing, he stumbled after me, his legs wobbling as we picked our way through the mud that surrounded the hall.

"I should get you to carry me over this," I said, pulling a stuck foot from a mud clutch, "but that's the sort of kind man I am."

"Y-yes, Brother Conrad," Brother Odo panted.

He believed me of course. The true reason for not having him carry me pig-a-back was that I wanted Brother Odo capable of speech when we found the monks of Medeshamstede. I pointed towards the church, a small wooden building with whitewashed walls some hundred yards from the king's hall.

"That's where we're going. The king is there, and our brothers from Medeshamstede."

Brother Odo suddenly stopped, a stricken look coming into his face.

"What's wrong?" I asked.

"They will not know," he said. "They will not know that the Danes burned the abbey and that the abbot and the rest of our brothers have been sold into slavery."

"Ah, yes, about that," I said. "Best not mention straight off that we sold the abbot and the brethren into slavery. Not until I've had a chance to explain the plan. You understand?"

49

Brother Odo nodded. "Indeed. If I did not know you for the good man that you are, I might think the worse: that you sold your brethren to gain a profit and that you have no intention of ever redeeming them. But while I know the true measure of you, my brothers here might not understand."

At these words, I looked sharply at Brother Odo, but there was nothing but honest acceptance, leavened with a good measure of exhaustion, in his eyes.

"That's true," I said. "Sometimes, we have to do that which we would not, so that good might come of it. Eventually."

"Yes, Brother Conrad."

We picked our way through the mud to the church and, finding the door open, entered. The king was there, kneeling in prayer before the altar, and on the altar, glittering and gleaming, was the Book.

Standing alongside the Book, next to the altar, were the three monks of Medeshamstede and, seeing Brother Odo enter the church, they rushed towards him, questions tumbling from their lips. But I saw that the king barely stirred as the monks went past him.

"Brother Odo and Brother…?" said the leading monk. I remembered his name if he did not know mine: Brother Gadd, a preening jackanape who took the foremost place in the choir for the sweetness of his voice and let no one forget it.

"Brother Conrad." My business was with the king. I looked to Brother Odo. "Tell them what happened."

While Brother Odo started to explain, his account interrupted by frequent exclamations of horror and invocations of the saints and angels, I made my way up the nave of the church to where the king still knelt in silent prayer before the Book. It was lifted up on a reading stand on the altar, open at the beginning of the Gospel according to St Matthew.

He did not stir at my approach, although he must surely have known, from the muffled but still discernible expostulations by the monks who had so recently abandoned their posts at the altar, that I brought news of some importance. But the king remained kneeling, his eyes fixed upon the Book, and he did not by so much as an alteration in his posture give any sign that he knew I was standing beside him.

Very few kings would remain thus in such uncertain times, when the word of travellers was fallen upon with all the ravenous eagerness of monks falling upon the Easter feast following the Lenten fast. But the king gave no sign that he kenned I was there, a stranger standing at his shoulder, and with none of his household within reach to defend him should I draw my seax and push it into the armpit in the killing strike.

However, my weapon of choice is words, not steel.

"My lord, I come with grave news."

Still the king did not stir. I glanced back at the monks, clustered around Brother Odo. Surely they would have told Brother Odo if the king had been seized by some sort of fit that rendered him incapable of speech and movement?

"My lord. King Edmund, I would speak with you if I may. I bring word from Abbot Flory and the monastery at Medeshamstede, whence came the Book you kneel before."

"Why do you not kneel before it?"

The words, coming from a face that had not once turned to acknowledge my presence, so disconcerted me that I had to ask the king to repeat them. He did, his face still turned to the Book and his body refusing to acknowledge my presence.

"Oh, yes, of course, my lord."

Getting down on my knees beside the king, I presumed he wanted me there so that he would not be talking up to me. I soon learned that this was not the case.

"My father's fathers came to this land and there was darkness in their souls and ignorance in their hearts. They passed from the mewling of babes to the drooling of gaffers with no more knowledge of what passed before their entry into this world and what would happen after they left it than a man, sitting huddled by the fire in my hall amid winter storms, knows when the storms shall pass. But in the time of my forefathers, knowledge came to us of these great mysteries, and a door was opened."

The king's face was shining as he spoke. I'd seen that sort of light before. It was an unearthly light, as if coming from some realm where the light was purer and more intense, but it always meant trouble.

King Edmund suddenly snapped his head round so that he was looking at me. "The knowledge is in this Book, and the gateway to our new life is by the bread and wine we eat. So what else should a king do than kneel before such wonders?"

I nodded. "Indeed, lord, indeed." To show I'd really got the message, I prostrated myself full length.

A moment later, the king joined me on the floor.

"I am not worthy even to raise my eyes to such wonders as are in the Book," I said, "although perhaps a king might gaze upon them and remain un-scorched."

King Edmund turned his eyes, that had widened in wonder, upon me.

"I thank you, Brother Monk, for you have truly schooled me in humility. For I thought myself worthy to look in adoration upon the Book of Life when, you are right, none of us may rightly even raise our eyes to it."

"Humility is the truest shield of the monk, as a good piece of lime-wood is the shield of the warrior."

"And the truth telling of his men is the best shield for a king." Edmund stood and then reached a hand down to me.

Although I did not betray my awareness of their scrutiny by so much as a flicker, I knew Brother Odo and the other three monks of the abbey were watching, with no little wonder, what was transpiring between me and the king, for a silence had fallen upon them where before there had been exclamations and cries of horror. Taking hold of the king's hand, I got to my feet.

Edmund looked me in the face with the searching scrutiny that kings favour. Since kings take pride in being able to read the secrets of a man's soul from the outside, I had spent much effort ensuring that when anyone subjected me to the truth stare, what they would see was the open and honest face of a man of worth and truth — and not the shifting mien of the vain dissimulator and crafty poltroon that I am.

So I met the king's gaze, my eyes clear, my chin raised and my brow untroubled, and he saw what I had put on show for him to see.

"I know," said King Edmund, after he had taken my measure, "that a man such as you would not interrupt me in vigil save for the most extreme need. So, tell me in what that need consists."

I endeavoured to maintain a regard of calm and courage — it is truly astonishing how little of the turmoil within it is possible to pass on to watching eyes — and spoke as quickly and simply as I might. Besides, anything longer and there was a rapidly increasing chance of my words dissolving into gibbering whimpers of fear.

"The Danes are coming."

The king nodded and his face showed no alarm, but behind him the faces of the three monks from Medeshamstede Abbey blanched.

"Yes, they would. I bought my people time when first they landed but I knew they would return. Like a dog to its vomit, the Dane returns whence he came." King Edmund looked at me. "How does he return?

With force or with demands?"

"The riders we saw following us were not enough to be vanguard for the Great Army, and they were travelling quickly — I think they bear message and, no doubt, demands."

The king nodded. "As I expected. They will seek to win this kingdom with words and threats and fear, rather than by the sword." Then, against all expectation, a brief smile lit the king's worn face. "Then that is how I shall meet them: with word and hope and a great promise."

Edmund was no young man. He could raise a harvest of grey hair from his beard and the age frost had touched his temples too. To have reached such an age with the crown still upon his head showed that Edmund must be a king of wit as well as strength, a man of subtlety sufficient to balance the ambitions of his thanes and his aldermen against each other, while maintaining a face turned to the other kingdoms that told of strength sufficient to dissuade others from reckless attack.

But if such wit and subtlety had kept his kingdom these many long years, it must have utterly deserted him in the face of the terror of the Northmen. For to think that words would turn aside the Great Army was as foolish as to think the tide might be stopped at a king's command.

It was a struggle, but my face was well trained: I affected a mien of supportive concern while reflecting inwardly that I would have to persuade this madman to give the Book into my keeping.

As Edmund made to go, I, apparently greatly daring, placed hand upon his shoulder to have him stay a moment longer.

He looked down upon my hand, but then turned to me, a mild smile upon his face, for I had confirmed for him that I was a man fearless and frank.

"You would speak further?"

"Only this, my lord. Flory, the abbot of the monastery at

Medeshamstede, sent me with my companion, Brother Odo, to bring the Book into a place of safety, that its knowledge and promise might not be lost, but rather be secure for the generations yet born."

The king, his eyes shining with a light that looked all too real to be comfortable, took my hands in his.

"But the Book will be safe here, far safer than if you took it into your keeping and fled. For then any party of marauding Danes might find you and kill you and defile the Book, thinking it only a treasure to break between them. But I shall wield the Book as it should be wielded, as the promise of hope everlasting, and I will lay this hope before the Danes and bring them to its knowledge." The king's smile grew broader and, to my eyes, madder. He was touched with the same lunacy that drove the monks from Ireland to cast themselves on to the sea in a boat with no oars, that the Lord might take them where he would, be that a new land at waters' end or the long prayer with the fishes of the deep.

"You will stand beside me as I call them to this new life and your quiet courage will be a surer witness to the triumph of our hope over fear of earthly death than any words of mine." He was squeezing my hands so hard now that all the blood was gone from them, but it was the pressure his words were putting on my heart that really hurt. The God light was in his eyes — and that was the light of madness. Somehow, I had to get away from the hall of this lunatic king before I was coiled into his plans. But I had to make my escape with the Book. I had no intention of becoming a wandering pauper, begging the gleaning of pigs from suspicious cottagers.

I smiled broadly.

"I will stand beside you, my lord, and together we shall summon the Danes to eternal life."

"Yes," said King Edmund. "I knew at once when I saw your face that here was a man who might understand that which I have been called upon to do. For my aldermen and my thanes, even the very men of my own household, do not understand. They all bid me either fight or flee. So when I tell them that I shall do neither, but give the Danes that which they do not have, they shake their heads and fall away from me." The king gestured through the body of the church towards his hall. "You see that which I am left with: men too old to seek another lord, or too young to leave their families. But I shall raise the promise up high before them and call them all to it."

The king let go my hands and took my arm.

"Let us go. With you beside me, I will meet these Danes."

Which was how I found myself standing on the platform that surrounded the king's great hall looking a battle-scarred Dane in the face.

King Edmund had waited there for the Danes with his threadbare collection of warriors and boys standing before him and one inwardly quaking companion at his shoulder. Brother Odo and the other monks of Medeshamstede had followed bringing, at the king's command, the Book with them. They now waited behind us, holding the Book concealed from view.

The king, I feared, intended to reveal the Book as his great weapon, a thing of beauty and knowledge to awe and inspire the Danes. Unfortunately, I knew all too well that the only awe it would inspire was awe at how much gold, silver and precious jewels had gone into its adornment, while knowledge of its presence here would only inflame the Danes' gold lust.

As we waited the approaching Danes, I ran through the possible outcomes in my mind: none of them were good, and most of them were disastrous. But as they drew closer the man around whom the column was arranged began to take on a disturbingly familiar aspect. The Great

Army had sent Thorgrim the Tall as its envoy. Of all the gold-hungry earls who quarrelled and argued and fought for precedence around the sons of Ragnarr, they would have to send the one who knew me.

Thorgrim drew his horse to a foam-splattered halt. His gaze went up and down the line of waiting men, identifying Edmund at a glance, then stopping for a moment at the sight of me, standing beside the king. Thorgrim settled his restive horse with word and hand, while I attempted to convey, by the earnest truthfulness of my expression, that I might be able to render some service to the Dane should he but pass in silence over my presence beside the king.

His horse quiet, Thorgrim turned his attention to the king. It seemed I had bought his present silence by the armfuls of gold I had earned him from the sale of the monks of the abbey.

"I bring message to Edmund, King of the East Angles, from the sons of Ragnarr: Ivarr, Ubba and Halfdan, the leaders of the Great Army of the Northmen that ravages your land." Thorgrim scanned the line of waiting men in calculated insult.

"If the king be here among you, let him stand forth."

At this, King Edmund laughed.

The sound, so unexpected, stopped Thorgrim more completely than the hiss of an arrow. The Dane's head snapped round and he looked to Edmund, laughing beside me.

"Why do you laugh?"

But so great was the king's laughter that all he could do for the moment was wipe the tears from his eyes. Behind Thorgrim, his riders shifted uncomfortably, eyes searching left and right. Surely such mirth betokened some unsuspected trap? I could see that even Thorgrim grew uneasy before such unnatural merriment, shifting upon his horse, eyes straining to remain upon the king when his back crawled at the fear of the unseen arrow's bite.

"Why do you laugh?" Thorgrim asked once more.

Now, at last, the king's mirth had subsided enough for him to essay answer. His eyes sparkling with the tears of glee, Edmund said, "I laugh, for you come to bid me hand over baubles and trinkets, nothing more than the playthings of babies, when I stand before you with a treasure greater than you imagine that you do not see."

"What treasure is this?" asked Thorgrim.

"Life," said the king. "I stand before you with life, and you see it not."

Earl Thorgrim's hand dropped to the hilt of his sword. Seeing this, Edmund's men tensed, hands going to their own swords, while spears were gripped ready.

But now it was the turn of the Danish earl to laugh.

"It seems your men are not so certain of this life you offer, or they would not stand so ready to fight for you." Thorgrim carefully raised his hand, so that all might see, and rested it in plain view upon the pommel of his saddle. "For my part, I will hear what you have to say after I have delivered that which I was sent to deliver."

"I fear I know all too well what you have been asked to deliver," said King Edmund.

"I would be the more surprised if you did not," said Thorgrim. "But let no man say I failed in the charge I was given. Here are the words I was bidden to speak to you by Ivarr and Ubba and Halfdan, the sons of Ragnarr Lothbrok. Listen well.

"To Edmund, King of the East Angles, greetings. You will have heard that which has come to pass since the year we spent in your kingdom, gathering our strength. Our strength waxed and, wielding it, we have cast down the kings of Northumbria and taken that ancient kingdom for our own. When we moved south, the king of Mercia, Burgred, attempted our defeat, but even with aid from the king of the West Saxons he could not defeat us and he paid us tribute in gold and silver. Burgred is now our vassal king. So, we return to you, Edmund of the East Angles, and give to you, for the sake of the service you did us before, this chance: that you may remain as king of the East Angles so long as you swear fealty to the sons of Ragnarr and, as sign of this, give to the keeping of the sons of Ragnarr your hidden gold hoards — for we know your kingdom to be rich and your land wealthy."

Thorgrim delivered his message with all the cross-eyed concentration of a messenger who has been required to recite the message many times in front of those sending it before he was allowed to depart. But having delivered his memorised message, the earl sat easy in his saddle and, looking down upon the king, smiled.

"For my part, I say it is a fair and just offer that the sons of Ragnarr make to you. They ask only that you acknowledge them as high kings, masters over this island."

"That, and our 'hidden gold hoards'," said Edmund. "Although where they think I might have hidden more gold, when they took so much from me when they first they came to this land, I do not know."

But Thorgrim waved his hand airily.

"For a king, there is always more gold. Will your people not offer their gold to you, for your continued rule and safety? I should think they would be happy to do so, if you are as beloved as people say."

"If they would, I would not accept it," said Edmund. "But we speak of trifles, when the great matter awaits — indeed, the matter before which all others pale."

I was standing beside Edmund as he spoke, and I saw that mad joy light in his eyes that I had seen before.

"I bid you take this word back to your masters, to Ivarr and Halfdan and Ubba. Tell them that I, Edmund, king of the East Angles, will submit to them, and submit to them right gladly..."

The king paused in his speech as the men around him breathed a collective gasp. But Edmund raised his hand, and all eyes turned to him, for there was in his face no sign of the defeat that his words signified.

"...I will submit to them as they must submit to the rightful lord of this land, whose word holds sway, whose promise gives hope, and whose body gives life. Let them submit to life in the King who is Christ, and I will, as brother, submit to them." Edmund smiled. "Tell them this, Earl Thorgrim: lest they submit to the God of my people and the Lord of this land, then their lives will be forfeit and their army wasted. Tell them, in our God is life: let them share it. Tell them: in their gods, there is only death. Tell them this too, Earl Thorgrim: that I put before them this day the blessing and the curse: therefore, let them choose life."

At the end of this peroration, everyone's face had turned towards Edmund. Everyone's, save mine. I was looking at Earl Thorgrim and the line of grim riders behind him. Yes, they were looking at Edmund too, but their faces were veiled and their eyes hooded; they had the look of hawks, standing upon the leather glove, waiting to be launched after their prey.

I thought I was the only one to read the predatory expressions on the faces of the Danes. Unfortunately, I was wrong. I had expected King Edmund, like a scop caught up in the music of his words, to be lost between the lines of thought. But he looked upon Thorgrim's face and saw there what I had seen and, seeing it, he did exactly what I had hoped he wouldn't. He turned to where Brother Odo stood with the monks of Medeshamstede and said to them, "Hold forth the Book, that these Danes without hope might see the hope we have."

I tried. I really did try to save the king from his stupidity. Before Odo and the other monks had time to lift the Book high to be venerated, I fell to the ground, thrashing my limbs and foaming at the mouth, thinking to set before the Danes the fear of the plague or the dropping sickness or some similar malady that might set them running. But the king took my diversion and fed it into his own madness. For he pointed at me, thrashing away and wondering how long I'd have to keep this up, and shouted, "See! The great holiness of the Book of Life robs even a holy monk such as Brother Conrad of power over his limbs. He shows us the way: let us all kneel in veneration before the source of hope and the promise of life!" And the king dropped to his knees, followed, with varying degrees of wariness, by his household retainers, who strove to keep one eye upon the Danes while keeping hands ready by swords.

Brother Odo and Brother Gadd raised the Book high.

I stopped thrashing around. I could have been lying there naked, humping a hog, and no one would have noticed.

The Book shone.

Held high, it caught the winter sun and it shone, as if a new sun had come down to this middle earth. The gold of its clasps and binding glowed as it must have glowed when poured from the smith's forge, while the garnets that studded the gold gleamed blood ruby with the life of the book.

It was the most magnificent sight I had ever seen. I turned from it and saw the lust in the eyes of the Danes, and I knew the Book was lost. Even if they did not take it now — and a rapid judgement suggested that the king's retainers outnumbered the Danes by too many for them to try to steal the Book as we spoke — yet the report of it, and the gold desire it had awakened in their loins, meant that Thorgrim would surely return with all the Great Army in his wake.

The Book was lost.

Unless I could save it.

"What — what is that?" asked Earl Thorgrim. Despite himself, he heeled his horse forward, as if he would grab the book from the monks. But the king's retainers closed ranks in front of Brother Odo, blocking Thorgrim's path.

"It is the Book of Life," said King Edmund. "Take word of its wonder back to the sons of Ragnarr, to Ivarr and Halfdan and Ubba, that they might know better the glory of the God who gave it to us, and lay aside the vain gods they follow and accept the God that rules in these lands. Then, tell them, they too would have a Book of Life such as this."

"This one?" said Thorgrim, pointing at the Book. "I — they — would have this book?"

"If not this, then its like," said the king.

But Thorgrim shook his head. "They will want *this* Book," he said. "No other."

"Then let them but accept our God, the God of this land, and I will give it to them," said Edmund. "Take word of this back to your lords, the sons of Ragnarr, Earl Thorgrim. Take word and tell its wonders and they will come to me."

"Oh, they will come," said Earl Thorgrim. "Do not think they won't, Edmund, king of the East Angles. They will come."

With that, he pulled the head of his horse and, heeling it, sent it off galloping back up the track in the direction whence he'd come, with his men following after.

We watched them out of sight, and then the king bent down to me and offered me his hand. I pulled myself up and attempted some explanation for why I had been struck down, but the king held up his hand.

"For the holy shall acknowledge the holy, and fall before it. In the short time I have known you, Brother Conrad, you have become an inspiration to me. Oh, that I could feel the lash of the sacred as you do, in your bowels."

I nodded, affecting the pained but enduring look of a man who felt the sacred deep in his bowels. From my observation, it is an expression similar to a man with piles settling himself astride a horse.

King Edmund, with his hand upon my shoulder, turned to his people.

"See the example of this man, Brother Conrad, newly come among us. See how that which is holy affects him. If we were all like that, the Danes would not dare to despoil us."

Not entirely to my surprise, there were some rumblings and mutterings of discontent among the king's retainers at these words. Rather more to my surprise, the king noticed them.

"Yes, yes, I hear your displeasure, my warriors. You have stood beside me through the long year of agony when the Danes made their camp among us, restraining yourselves from repaying anger to insult, at my command waiting, always waiting, and never raising sword to avenge insult. Now, we will feast, for the great day approaches of our deliverance."

It was as well that my head was bowed in modest appreciation of the praise the king had bestowed upon me, or those watching would have seen the desperate fight I waged to keep the despair from my face. The king would face the Danes armed with nothing more lethal than a book. We were all going to die.

"So, I bid you, rejoice and be glad. Do not be afraid, for He who lives is with us." The king beckoned his steward to him and, since I was standing on his other side, I heard the quiet instructions he gave the man. There was to be nothing held back for store. The steward was to prepare a feast for all, and he was to use everything.

To my ears, this sounded like a funeral feast.

Chapter 5

I reckoned on having three, maybe four days before the Great Army arrived. By then, I needed to have got hold of the Book and departed with it to a more secure location, preferably over the sea. To that end, while the steward set about preparing the feast the king had proclaimed, I made the acquaintance of the horse master, passing a long hour with him casting my eyes over horse flesh while he rambled on interminably about shanks and fetlocks and all those bits of a horse that keep a horse master's mind occupied, while I decided which of this collection of broken-down nags was least likely to collapse under me during a chase.

Listening to the horse master's complaints, I learned that my judgement of the king's horses —that most were barely fit to be pack animals — was matched by his own. It seemed that the king's finest horses were lost to him during the Great Army's long stay, as supposed guests, in his kingdom, when the sons of Ragnarr had bought for derisory sums the best animals from the king's stables. With the kingdom swept clear of every good horse, this collection of hacks, nags and broken-down ponies was the best that he could assemble for the king's use.

Even to my untutored eye, it was obvious that none of these animals could be relied upon to carry me swiftly to safety, particularly if pursued by a group of angry warriors set on reclaiming a missing book. So, with the horse master's complaints still whining in my ear, I left and made my way back to the great hall. I would have to come up with a better plan than swipe and ride.

But as I walked towards the hall, I saw one of the slaves, a girl of fresh face and reasonably clean hair, bending over to wash the spoons in a bowl, her blouse hanging open enough for me to see the curve of her breast. Sensing my regard, she looked up and, seeing my look, flashed a quick smile as she tightened her blouse.

Being an austere monk of ascetic bent, I naturally looked away — but only after returning her smile with the added, agonised suggestion of desire inflamed but thwarted by my vows. I had three or four days before the Great Army arrived. I would not need all that time to plan my escape with the Book.

I glanced back. The slave girl was looking after me. I looked away, feigning embarrassment. I did not have to look again to know the face of smug satisfaction that she would be wearing. The problem was, she belonged to the king. I could not simply take her. Nor could I ask Edmund for use of her, not when he thought me a holy ascetic.

But maybe I could ask her for another...

I found the king alone in his hall. All around, there was the rush of slaves preparing the feast, but Edmund sat alone at the high table.

Never before had I seen this: a king left unattended in his hall. From waking to sleeping, a king is subject to the calls and demands of his people: I remember seeing King Burgred, squatting over his toilet while hearing the case of a churl against his neighbour for ploughing over his land. The king had squeezed out a judgement as he squeezed out his bowels. Indeed, the only time a king is not in public, he's expected to be producing young æthelings with his queen. So to see Edmund sitting at the high table with no one pressing suit or claim or question upon him was to see a wonder.

"My lord."

The king looked round to me, as if surprised that anyone should speak to him.

"They are preparing the feast."

"Yes," said Edmund. His eyes were on the rush in front of him, but he was looking at something far beyond. "It will be my last, I think."

"Surely not, my lord."

The king smiled. "They sense it. Death's shroud lies over my head and about my shoulders; it waits simply to be wound around my body. The living shun the presence of the dead. That is why I sit here, alone, amid many." Then the king turned his face towards me. "You alone come to sit with a dead man, Brother Conrad. I thank you for keeping company with me through this hour."

I nodded, but said no more, and waited.

"It is strange, to come to this autumn of my life, and find myself alone. None of the men I thought near to me understand. The queen speaks only to her women and turns her face from me. None see the necessity of what I must do. But you understand, don't you, Brother Conrad? That must be why God sent you here, in my extremity, that I be not alone in what I must do."

"Yes, my lord." I did not know what he was talking about, but by agreeing I might find out. Besides, the more often I said yes, the more likely he would be to say yes when I asked him for something — or someone.

"Come, sit beside me, Brother Conrad. I would speak with someone through this long watch."

Sitting down next to him, I looked at the preparations. "Surely, it will not be long before the feast begins, lord."

Edmund shook his head. "The long watch of which I speak is the watch beside the dead." He looked into the hall but again, his eyes saw other things than a room full of bustling slaves and worried warriors. "My thanes and my aldermen, my warriors and my queen, they all speak askance of that which I propose. They tell me it is madness to think that the sons of Ragnarr will put aside their idols and demons and accept the hope we have. But was it not madness for Paulinus and Augustine, for Aidan and Cedd to come before our forefathers unarmed save for the promise of life? Our forefathers turned aside from their idols, they put away the demons they had worshipped and accepted the truth. Why should the Danes not do likewise, when the choice is laid before them?" The king turned to look at me and his eyes were haunted.

I began to speak, then held my tongue. For I realised, to my surprise, that the fear in his eyes was not the fear of death, but the fear of failure.

"Surely, in this as in all things, God's will shall be done," I said. "It is but our task to open before the Northmen the door to life; but as with a donkey, we can take them to the living water but we cannot make them drink it."

King Edmund nodded, slowly. "You speak wisely, Brother Conrad. Some call me fool for essaying such a thing. Others, without word, have gone from my court and my household, saying no farewell." Edmund leaned closer to me so that others might not overhear. "By Heaven, I can find it in my heart to place no blame upon them, for I fear their charge be true. It is a fool's gamble and a child's play: the hope of a king shorn of power." A spasm of pain passed over the king's face at his memory of that dark year. "I sacrificed my people's trust, and their treasure, to hold the throne for a year and a year again." Edmund opened his eyes and looked upon me, and his face was dark with memory. He grasped my arm. "Know this then, good and holy Brother Conrad. Hear my deepest, darkest hope. My counsellors and my aldermen — who are often not the same thing — are in one matter at least agreed: the king's madness." Edmund's grip on my arm tightened, his fingers digging into my forearm as if he was a man clutching for life against the cold tug of a river current. "None of them believe that the Danes will heed my call and abandon their gods for our God. They think me a fool, or mad."

Abruptly, the king released my arm. I thought, at least the king's counsellors and aldermen were not fools or lunatics. I had better keep clear of them.

"They are right." The king turned his gaze back upon me. "I *am* mad and a fool. The sons of Ragnarr will not heed my call; they will turn their back upon life and choose death. I know this, as you know this, wise and holy Brother Conrad. But that is not the basis of my hope. Mine is a terrible hope, and I shrink before it, Brother Conrad. I fear I have not the strength to carry it out. In the dark of my heart, I pray that this cup might pass from me. Do you understand what I am saying?" The king took my hand in his. "Do you?"

I nodded. "Yes," I said. "Yes, I understand." Of course, I did not have any idea what he was talking about, but I was confident that he would tell me.

"I would speak of this to no one else, but I speak of it with you because you of all men might stay and share this cup with me. Will you do that, Brother Conrad? For I fear, in my weakness, that I do not have the courage to drain this cup on my own. But if you were to stay with me, then I would draw strength from your courage, and hope from your faith, and we might together accomplish what I fear I cannot do alone. Will you do this, Brother Conrad?"

This is the problem of dealing with a madman. Sometimes, he will think you know what he is talking about and expect you to answer accordingly. However, a madman seldom remembers the promises of yesterday on the morrow.

Placing my other hand on his, I joined our hands in a pact of flesh. "Yes, my lord. I will stay and we will accomplish your hope together."

The king bowed his head. I could see his lips moving. He was praying. When he lifted his head, his eyes were shining, but this was the sheen of tears.

"I had prayed the Lord would send me someone to strengthen me in faith and to aid me in the trials I will face, and he has answered me beyond all hope! Together, we will face the Danes and we will offer ourselves as living sacrifices for our people, in atonement for their sins, that God's wrath be turned aside and his just vengeance be visited on us. I had thought I would have to face this alone but now, you are here, I know that there will be someone to suffer alongside me. I am content." His eyes still shining, the king's tears fell from his cheek and landed on my hands. "We will enter Heaven together, Brother Conrad. What greater bond of brotherhood can there be than that?"

So, the king's plan was to offer himself as a sacrifice to the Danes in expiation for the sins of his people, and I was now going to be part of that sacrifice, too.

Under the circumstances, I think I did rather well. My hands did not tighten uncontrollably, nor did my bowels loosen to any extent appreciable to onlookers. I no doubt paled, but with the firmness of my jaw it looked to be the firmness of stern decision rather than the rictus of fear it was. I even managed a nod of acceptance. But no speech. I have learned that, of all parts of the body, the voice is the one most likely to betray me when I am in great fear. So I refrained from speech, and merely nodded.

"We must shrive ourselves of sin," the king went on. "For though a martyr's death is a sure entrance to the lord's great hall, we must not go in stained with the dirt of this middle earth. I will call my priest to hear and shrive us before I summon the rest of the court to leave."

"Y-you don't want anyone else to stay?" I asked, with only quite a small tremor to my voice.

"No. I, as king, shall offer myself in sacrifice for my people if the Danes will not put aside their idols. You, as a holy son of the Church, shall be her sacrifice for the conversion of these heathens and the salvation of this land. After the feast, I shall order all the court to leave us. We will face the Danes together, unarmed and alone." The king smiled. "I at least am more fortunate than Our Lord. He had to face his accusers alone, for all his retainers abandoned him. But you, I know, will not abandon me."

I shook my head. "No, lord, I would never do that." I dropped my voice, so that others might not hear. "How long before the Danes arrive?"

"Three or four days. We will have time for my funeral feast." He smiled. "And yours."

"Thank you, lord. That is… thoughtful of you." Under the circumstances, my voice was holding up quite well, I thought. "When will you send your household away?"

"As soon as our funeral feast is over."

"So, we will be alone here for a day or two?"

"Yes, I expect so. You will sustain me in prayer and fasting, Brother Conrad, while we await our martyrdom."

I nodded. It would surely be possible to escape this mad king's company once his hearth companions had left. And with only Edmund to guard the Book, I should have little difficulty obtaining it for myself. In fact, the king's lunacy was playing out to my advantage.

Under the circumstances, I decided to enjoy myself further. Still, this would need to be done with tact. I tapped the king on his hand, and whispered in reply to his questioning look.

"There is one who might ask a favour of you, lord."

Edmund looked knowingly at me, but I shook my head. "No, no, it is not for *me*. The only favour I ask is to share your trial and to win the red crown of martyrdom alongside you. But it is indeed true, what you said, about the weakness of the flesh, and though I myself have mortified my fleshly desires such that I can look upon a woman unclothed and be unmoved, yet there are others who still labour under the sting of the flesh, and seek release from its urgings."

Edmund nodded. "I am young enough to remember that myself."

"Besides, it is said that a man might face the dangers of the morrow more calmly when he has eased the pangs of the flesh in the night."

"So some say," said the king.

"Then perhaps my lord might see fit to allow my servant, Odo, to ease the nerves of his flesh with one of your slaves this night?" I pointed to the slave girl whom I'd marked earlier. She was serving at one of the tables, slapping off the attentions of the men sitting there. "Such a one might be suitable."

"But surely your servant is a monk professed, forsworn from the flesh?"

"Ah, that is how I have had him appear," I said, "for in these troubled times it were better that two monks travel together than I go with a servant abroad. But he is but my servant, a man of flesh, and since I will likely have need of him in the days ahead it would be a great service to me, lord, if you would take away this distraction from him."

Edmund, however, shook his head. "If it were anything else you asked, I could surely say yes, and gladly. But it is the custom of this court that even those who are held as slaves among us are not forced

EDOARDO ALBERT

against their will into the beds of free men. However, if she will go freely to your man, then I will turn my eyes away, even though it were better at this time for him to think on things eternal than that which shall surely perish. But you are right: few can find the strength to turn from the flesh, even when death waits upon us."

"You are merciful, my lord, as I knew you would be, but you are right: I will tell Odo to master his desires and turn his mind to eternal things and away from the flesh."

The king nodded. "That were indeed better." He pointed to the doors to the kitchen, which were flung wide as the first of a long procession of servers entered the hall. "The feast is about to begin."

It was the strangest feast I have ever attended. Wine, beer, ale and mead flowed in quantities I had seldom seen, and was drunk with a grim, concentrated determination. The food never seemed to end, although it was plain fare: the steward, given little time to prepare for the feast, had only been able to prepare the simplest dishes, but the entire contents of the king's stores were laid out before us by the end of the evening.

And through almost all the feast, the king sat alone, a man apart, like a corpse laid out before his people, and few dared even to raise their eyes to him. Slipping out of the hall to relieve myself, I spied the slave girl I had asked the king about and called her over.

"My lord?"

The way she said that, raising her eyes to mine then dropping her gaze, almost made me throw aside discretion there and then. It had been a while since I had been anywhere near a maid of such beauty — although judging by the half smile that twitched at her lips, she was no maid.

"What is your name?"

"Sexburh, my lord."

"A Saxon fortress? I trust, if the king commands it, you will not

72

defend your fortress too vigorously?"

"It would depend on who was besieging the fortress, my lord."

"But if the king commands?"

"If the king commands it, I would, I suppose, have to surrender the fortress in the end, my lord." She raised her face to me, and I suddenly realised that word of my desire would be spread among the slaves of the king's household before even I had chance to slake it. It is said that news among slaves in the morning reaches the king's ear by the evening. Although Edmund was sending everyone away on the morrow, could I risk him hearing of my nocturnal exploits? Everything depended on him thinking me a holy and pious monk. That reputation would be grievously damaged if he learned that I'd tumbled one of his slave girls during the night.

Time for some misdirection.

"Oh," I laughed, "you don't think…?" I laughed again. "No, no, not me. The king commands you to surrender your fortress to my slave — it is a favour I asked of him."

"Your slave?" asked Sexburh.

"Yes, yes. Odo. Ha, I really think you thought I was asking for myself. No, it's for Odo. But he is shy, so he wants you to wait for him somewhere dark, where you will not see him unclothed." I pointed to one of the sheds that surrounded the king's hall. "That one. After the feast, he will come to you. Make sure it's dark."

"Dark." Sexburh nodded. She wasn't looking at me any longer, but then I had disappointed her. After all, she had thought she was getting me, now she believed it would be Brother Odo. Still, this way I could have her and protect my name with the king.

"Don't you forget," I said. "In the shed, after the feast. No candle or lamp, or the king will be displeased."

"Yes, lord," said Sexburh. She did not look up at me. "Is that all?"

"Yes. Run along now." I watched her go, enjoying the way her rump moved beneath her clothes. As far as I was concerned, the feast couldn't end soon enough.

But of course it dragged on and on, as these things do, with maudlin warriors staring into their cups and telling tearful tales of comrades lost and battles won, while the king's scop went from telling the tale of Edmund's heroic forebears through songs of war and dragon-haunted peace to drunken riddles and, finally, blessed incoherence, as his fingers missed the strings of the lyre and his tongue fought a losing battle with his ale-addled wits; he sank into a snoring heap by the fire, a sleep from which not even a volley of thrown bones could wake him.

Through most of the feast, the king sat alone. It had begun with the queen asking him to think again about his decision to send her away on the morrow. When Edmund refused, the queen had withdrawn with her women, returning to her own apartment. At intervals throughout the feast, various counsellors had made representations to the king, speaking quietly to him, but always his response had been to shake his head — and, usually, to give them a ring or a brooch until, by the latter part of the feast, the king had no more gifts of gold to give.

I would have been concerned about this disposal of the king's wealth, if my desire had lain elsewhere than the Book. But next to the Book, all the arm rings and brooches and buckles Edmund was passing to his old and faithful retainers were no more than baubles and trinkets. I watched the gold glitter assuaging the guilt of retainers being asked to abandon their lord, its yellow lustre painting over the dark shame in their eyes. These were men brought up to believe that the noblest act of all was to die in a heap of hewn flesh around the fallen body of their lord.

Even as a boy, I had thought that all to be nonsense. Surely it made more sense to get away, intact and whole, and then return later to wreak vengeance for your fallen lord on his killers? Then, when I had known battle and war for themselves, and not just through the songs of the scops, I had realised that the only glory in battle was living through it, and the best plan of all was to make sure I was somewhere else entirely when the shieldwalls clashed. For I had seen the best warriors, men skilled and strong, brought down by a rock over which they stumbled, or the fear of a friend, breaking the wall and leaving their shield mate exposed. Skill, strength, courage: none of them mattered a jot in battle compared to fortune's favour. And the greatest favour fortune could bestow, and one with which I co-operated wholeheartedly, was to avoid battle altogether.

But to the king's men, Edmund's concern for their lives seemed like their disgrace. When some of the older and more decrepit retainers shed tears on to his outstretched hands and begged to be allowed to stay and die alongside him, it was with some little difficulty that I restrained myself from telling them their stupidity. I quietened my tongue and contented myself with watching Sexburh move between the benches, slapping away the hands of the warriors who reached for her while filling their cups with ale and beer. But I noticed that she never went to the table where Brother Odo sat with the other monks of Medeshamstede, and if she ever looked to him, it was a passing glance.

The feast finally dwindled into drunken snores and unsettled sleep. Men lay sprawled on bench and table, dogs twitched contentedly, their bellies filled with fallen scraps and snatched treats, and the air was thick with the smell of spilled beer and heavy with smoke: it was like the aftermath of every other feast I had attended over the years. Towards the end, a few men had slipped furtively from the hall, following after a promising glance from a girl, and outside I heard some quiet giggles and short bursts of rapid breathing.

Sexburh was helping to clear up, but I caught her eye from where I sat, and held her glance for a moment. Brother Odo and the other monks, having taken little drink, were sitting in quiet conversation. She glanced to them, sighed and gave me a quick nod. Then she slipped from the hall.

I thought on whether I should reveal myself to her. It would make the tumble the better if she realised she was tupping me, rather than Brother Odo. But then, what surety did I have that she would not boast afterwards? No, better to go hooded, and as Brother Odo. If she should prove particularly pleasing, and I should want to go round again, then perhaps I would let her know who I was. But, for now, my blood grew hot. It was as well, when I stood, that my robe hung loose. I made towards the door.

"My friend, where go you?"

I turned to see the king, whom I had thought asleep, beckoning to me.

"My lord, I must needs relieve myself. I will return as soon as I may."

"Be quick. I would speak with you this lonely night."

Well, that settled it, I thought, as I hurried out of the great door. It would have to be quick.

With the torches flaring and guttering around the great door, I could see the dark shape of the hut where I had told Sexburh to wait on Brother Odo. I hurried towards it, loosening my trousers as I went. Opening the door, I saw, from the faint light of the torches, a pale suggestion of a face peering over rough blankets on the floor. Normally, with a girl as comely as Sexburh, I would have stopped to admire her form, but I was in a hurry. Pushing the door closed behind me, I dropped my trousers and lay atop her.

Considering she thought I was Brother Odo, Sexburh was surprisingly enthusiastic, although for a girl of her youth, her skin was a little rougher than I had expected.

"You — you might have washed first," I gasped.

But Sexburh just laughed. Her voice was hoarser than I had remembered, but then, pleasure makes many women sound hoarse, and from the way she was thrashing beneath me, she was enjoying this as much as me. Trouble was, it had been many weeks, and I was in a hurry. The tumble became a fall, and ended for me all too quickly. I made to get up.

"Oh, don't stop, darling. I'm just getting started."

Half standing and pulling up my trousers, I froze. That voice. That voice did not sound like Sexburh's voice.

Slowly, I opened the door. With my eyes adjusted to the darkness in the hut, the light I let in illuminated everything. It illuminated everything all too well.

Sitting up on the blanket was a crone, snaggle toothed and wart ridden, her dugs hanging down to her waist. She reached out towards me. "Come on, darling. I'm ready for more."

Horrified, I backed towards the door and, as I did so, I heard from behind me clear, girlish laughter.

"Old Luba fancied a tumble to remind her of when she was young, so I swapped with her, Brother Monk. I hope you don't mind."

Drawing my hood over my head, I turned and ran back towards the hall, the joined laughter of Sexburh and Luba following me as I went. Before re-entering the hall, I found a bucket of water and washed as thoroughly as I might those parts of me that had been most intimate with old Luba. The water was mortifyingly cold, but it could not banish the shock of what I had seen — and done.

Chapter 6

"I don't understand it," Brother Odo told me the next morning. "All the slaves keep looking at me, and pointing and laughing. Did I say something funny in my sleep?"

"How would I know?" I said. I was, I admit, feeling tetchy this morning. But then I realised that Brother Odo's question meant that the slaves thought it had been him last night, not me. My disguise had worked, even if I had been tricked into tupping a crone. Feeling somewhat better, I turned my morning growl into a smile and turned back to Brother Odo. "One of the slaves, a woman called Luba, might be able to help with your question. Why don't you ask for her?"

My lonely breakfast was subsequently greatly brightened by watching Odo go to a slave, ask after Luba, and be directed, after a fit of laughter, out of the hall. Indeed, so much was I enjoying it all that I followed. Blinking in the cold morning light, I saw the wagons and donkeys, the oxen and horses that signified a royal court about to move. Men were packing wagons, others were unloading store sheds and leading beasts made irritable by all the noise and movement to where they were needed. Amid all the confusion, I saw Brother Odo latch on to another passing slave and, judging by the broad smile on the slave's face, ask after Luba again. This time he was pointed towards the steward's wagons. Shaking his head in continuing puzzlement, Brother Odo went where he was directed. For a moment I thought of following, so that I could witness close up the meeting between the lovers. But then I thought again: did I really want to see Luba, up close and in daylight? I'd had enough difficulty getting to sleep last night with her shadow shrouded features in my memory. She was not likely to look better in this cold winter light.

So I remained where I was, while slaves and retainers rushed to and fro, watching Brother Odo's progress from a distance. Even amid the noise of leaving, it was easy to mark wherever he asked after Luba from the crow of laughter that followed in his wake, and the pointing fingers. Indeed, among this sombre leaving, the laughter following Brother Odo was the only merriment to be heard.

Usually, when it comes time for a king to leave his estate and move on to the next hall, there is great joy among his retinue. It is a time of leaving; young warriors sneak off to make final farewell to the local girls they have impressed, leaving honey promises that they will remain true until next the king's caravan passes this way. But there was none of that this time. Only dour faces, setting about a grim task that had been commanded of them.

Of the king, there was no sign.

Then I realised where he must be. The church. Edmund would be in prayer. I should join him; not just to cement my reputation for holiness but to ensure that the monks Abbot Flory had sent with the Book did not remain when the king's household departed.

But first, Brother Odo.

I heard another burst of laughter, looked to see a hand pointing, a wagon cover flung open and, even over the hubbub of the leaving, a voice crying, "Lover, you came back!" Brother Odo was being pulled, as stricken as a hen before a stoat, into the back of the wagon. I watched, counting, "One, two, three, four, five..." On five, the wagon exploded open once more and Brother Odo emerged, running, his robes dishevelled and his face redder than a beetroot, amid raucous laughter from the surrounding men and women, and with Luba peering from the back of the wagon, beckoning him, and screeching, "Lover, come back!" Brother Odo came scampering back to the hall, his robes pulled up to his thighs to ensure he wouldn't fall over and be dragged back into the clutches of Luba.

"She — she wanted...she said I had..."

I patted Brother Odo on the back. "You really will have to get control of this sleep walking."

"What? You don't think...?"

"And by the sound of it, not just sleep walking but sleep..."

"No! No, I swear it. Ask brothers Gadd, Chad and Ræd."

"Oh, *I* believe you," I said. "But I'm not sure *they* do." And I pointed back towards Luba's wagon, where the old crone was waving after Brother Odo while regaling an interested party of listeners with her exploits of the night.

"You — you've got to tell them it isn't true," said Brother Odo. "They will believe you."

"Would you? In my experience, given a good story or a boring truth, people will always choose to believe the story. The only way to get them to change what they think is to give them an even juicier story. Maybe we could say that brothers Gadd, Chad and Ræd took turns with Luba last night. The gossips would enjoy that, and the old crone would like as not be flattered."

"No, no, I can't do that," said Brother Odo, "that would be lying. No monk would break his God oath like that."

"Indeed, quite right," I said. "But unfortunately, with such an uncouth crowd of slaves, no one is going to believe you. So best leave it. After all, they'll all be gone in a few hours." I patted Brother Odo on the back. "Come with me. It's time we found the king."

*

By the time the sun had laboured up as high in the sky as it was going to go at this season, the king's household had departed.

Edmund stood before the doors of his hall, waving to them as they left, and their leaving was long. Fortunately some stomach gripes helped me look pinchedly holy. At my request, the king had allowed Brother Odo to stay, although he played no part in the farewell: fearful that Luba would make another grab for him, he spent the whole time hiding in the hall, occasionally peering out timidly to see if she had gone. I saw Sexburh leave, walking alongside the queen's wagons, her hips swinging when she saw my eye upon her. Thunor's bollocks, seeing her, I wished the harder the little doxy had not fooled me. When she cast a parting glance in my direction I promised myself that, once I got out of here with the Book, I'd claim the night she owed me.

As for the monks of Medeshamstede, they left with the king's household. I pointed out that their duty now was to the abbey, or what was left of it. They had to go back and re-establish the work of monks; with three of them, there was enough to say the Office and do the work of prayer that was a monk's allotted task. Besides, Abbot Flory had given charge of the Book to me, and I was staying with the king to look after it — and to face the Danes.

Faced with the choice of remaining true to the Book or the Office, brothers Gadd, Chad and Ræd, being sensible monks, chose to leave rather than risk being fitted for the red crown of martyrdom.

My main concern, once this matter was settled, was to ensure that in the noise and confusion of the leave taking, I managed to sequester a donkey for my later use. I already had my horse, but I would need a beast to carry supplies. In this task, Brother Odo proved useful, since I engaged the horse master in a wager on the truth of Luba's tale and sent Brother Odo to him to swear his innocence. As I had expected, blush that had accompanied the oath taking meant that the horse master regarded himself as the winner of the wager, and I paid with apparent ill grace. But the couple of pennies I lost were more than worth the diversion, as it allowed one of the less trustworthy stable lads to hide an old donkey in a shed for my later use. The lad left with his couple of pennies, the horse master drove his beasts ahead while looking at the still blushing Brother Odo and mimicking acts that made Odo blush all the deeper, and I had my escape set up.

Now, it was just a case of waiting until the king's household had put enough distance between themselves and us, and then it would be time to leave. That meant the rest of the day and the morrow, although it would be cutting fine the time before the Danes arrived.

If I had thought the leaving of the king's household was tedious, I was wrong. The morning, in comparison to the afternoon, was a cavalcade of diversions. When the last of the stragglers disappeared into the distance and the king finally lowered a hand that had been raised for the best part of six hours, I naturally expected us to repair inside the hall to break our fast.

Not a bit of it. The king intended to fast until the Danes arrived. I pointed out that, since we were already intending to sacrifice ourselves, it seemed a little excessive to sacrifice our stomachs beforehand, but Edmund did not listen. He was all but running to the church — indeed, for the last few steps he did run. Bursting through the door, he then stopped and stared up at the altar with the sort of rapture I'd felt when, as a youth, I'd found out that the Lady Godgifu, my father's new, young and extremely pretty bride, was not so lady-like after all.

"In all the hours left to me, I will not be parted from this Book, nor will I leave this holy house." Edmund fell to his knees. I followed, more circumspectly (nothing being more calculated to slow down an escape than bad knees). The king began to shuffle up the nave to the altar on his knees, singing psalms — in atrocious Latin — as he went.

Knee walking is not easy. I attempted to follow but when my tunic got caught under my knee for the third time, I got up and followed, in a manner considerably more stately and dignified than the king, as he made his slow progress to the altar.

Having got to the altar, we then spent the rest of the afternoon on our knees before it. Edmund sang psalms, said prayers out loud with sighs and lamentations, or prayed in silence, when only the tears tracking down his cheeks told the depth of his prayers. Thankfully, the king was almost completely absorbed in his devotions and seldom looked round to see if I was still there. It was not too difficult for me, at those times, to affect a suitably prayerful attitude, although the increasing growling from my stomach betrayed my hunger.

In the end, Edmund either took pity on me, or found the noise too distracting.

"The spirit is willing but the flesh is weak," he said, his eyes still raised to the altar. "Go and eat, my friend, and then return and keep vigil with me."

I signalled to Brother Odo, who was kneeling at the back of the church, to follow me. He left but, for the first time, he showed some displeasure at my command, his face grimacing when he saw my gesture.

As we made our way towards the hall I asked him of this. In my experience, it's always best to stamp on the first sign of disobedience from a slave (yes, I know that by canon law Odo was not my slave, but since he was my junior in religion, he was my slave if I chose that for him). In answer Brother Odo, evidently mortified, went down on his knees before me.

"I beg your forgiveness, Brother Master." This 'Brother Master' was a new appellation but, since it nicely summed up our relationship, I was happy to let it pass into his usage without further comment. "I was so wrapped in prayer, I let that for a moment stop me following my oath of obedience to you. I shall mortify myself." And he began slapping himself round the face.

"No, no need for that," I said, grabbing his arm before he could knock himself out. Besides, I needed him to go and scout if there was any sign of the approaching Great Army. So, while I occupied myself with working through the provisions the steward had left behind, Brother Odo rode out from the king's settlement atop the donkey, with strict orders to come back by nightfall, and stricter orders to outrun the donkey if he saw any sign of the Danes.

Suitably sustained, and with a couple of flat loaves strapped to my knees to act as cushions, I went back to the church. Edmund was still there, still on his knees, his eyes still fixed upon the Book on the altar. But when I took my position next to him, he looked to me, and I saw the tears upon his cheeks and the strain upon his face.

"My fears grow great about me," he said, "and my heart is heavy. Without your quiet strength to sustain me, I prayed that God might take this cup from me. I felt so alone. I am not worthy of you, my friend."

"There are times when even the bravest soul must cry out, 'My God, my God, why have you forsaken me?' But the brave soul, crying out, endures. I will keep watch with you, my lord, and by each other's presence we will know that God has not forsaken us."

"Thank you, thank you." The king took my hand, and kissed it. And that's how we spent the rest of the day. The bread knee cushions proved their worth: not only did they protect my knees, but they provided sustenance through that endless afternoon and longer evening.

Finally, as the sun set, the king rose from his knees. I followed, more slowly and more stiffly.

"I would not be away from here," said Edmund, "so I must ask this of you, Brother Conrad. Will you go and bring me some bread, and small beer? The Lord has put it in my mind that I do not know for sure how many days it will be before the Danes come, and I would not be unmanned before them from lack of food. But I will not leave the Book untended."

"I would be more than glad to watch the Book if you would go and eat, my lord," I said.

But the king shook his head. "No, it is my part to remain with the Book always and never leave it from my sight so long as my eyes look out upon this middle earth."

Leaving the church, I saw Brother Odo returning. Since he was riding the donkey rather than running before it, I assumed that there was, as yet, no sign of the Great Army, a fact that Brother Odo confirmed when he dismounted.

"Can I go and pray with the king?" he asked me after he had given his report.

"Don't you want something to eat first?"

But Brother Odo shook his head. "I shall have food, and food in abundance, in God's kingdom. For now, my stomach can wait."

My stomach grumbled in answer.

"But you, Brother Master, should eat. It were not good that you grow weak through hunger — it says that in our Rule."

"Yes, yes of course. I will bring the king something too."

While Brother Odo and the king prayed, I made the preparations for my departure. My horse, while of no breeding, was a sturdy enough beast. I made sure it had to eat and drink, and then prepared supplies for myself that I laid in readiness in the stable with the horse. That done, I made a meal for myself, and a good one, before returning to the church with the requested bread and small beer.

I was sure that Edmund would want to spend the night in the church. But even a king so devout as Edmund would need to sleep, and I intended to leave with the Book when it was my turn to keep vigil.

But the king did not sleep.

Frankly, it was a shame that Jesus did not take Edmund, king of the East Angles, to the Garden of his agony, rather than Peter and James and John. There would have been no complaints from him then about being left alone through that night. Instead, through the long dark watch, with the winter cold seeping in through the walls of the church and leeching the warmth from my bones, I knelt before the Book and listened for the change in breathing that would indicate that Edmund finally slept. Admittedly, that was rendered more difficult by Brother Odo's snoring.

He had sworn he would keep watch through the night too, and had begun it on his knees with us. But then his head had drooped, nodded, drooped again, before his body slowly subsided to the ground, like a candle with an untrimmed wick burning down on one side. Now he lay on his side, muttering occasionally — usually some panicked cry of "No, Luba, I won't," — and snoring more often. At least his snoring was gentle, akin to the purring of kittens, rather than the honking rasps that I had had to put up with when I was put in the monastery dormitory next to Brother Aculf. When Brother Tidgar, the novice master, refused to move me, I led a sleep-walking Brother Aculf to Brother Tidgar's cot and got him to climb in next to him. That got Brother Aculf moved quickly enough, as well as earning him three years of penitential baths in ice water. Seeing as how he was now the property of Fat Rolf, Brother Aculf's life had probably taken a turn for the better, at least so far as his ice-shrivelled member was concerned.

But my member, not to mention my fingers, toes, nose and ears, were losing all feeling while beside me, Edmund kept up a steady litany to the saints.

"Saint Tertullian..."

"...pray for us."

"Saint Alban..."

"...pray for us."

"Saint Severian..."

"...pray for us."

I mean, who would believe there was ever a St Severian? What sort of name is that? I began to suspect that the cold had addled the king's wits and he was just making up names and putting 'saint' in front of them. Who would know? But at one point, when the dark was deepest and I could barely even see his shadow, he almost made me jump to my feet by reaching out to touch me. Indeed, I'm sure I would have shrieked and jumped up, if my lips had not been so numb and my limbs so stiff.

"Can you feel them?" the king had asked me. "They are all around us, adding their prayers to ours."

"Y-yes," I'd chattered. "I can feel them t-too."

"All the host of Heaven's army is gathered round us: saints and angels, archangels and cherubim, seraphim and principalities, dominations, thrones and powers. They are all here, with us, in the dark, and it is not dark any longer, but bright with their light."

"I-I can hardly see, it's so bright."

"For the holy, all is light."

At that, I maintained a modest silence. But all those saints and angels must have eventually left, for the litany died away and we dragged through the hours in silence, with me listening for any rustle or sigh to indicate that the king was finally flagging.

And, at last, it came.

A sound like a basket of rushes being emptied upon the floor. Looking round, I saw the dark puddle of Edmund's shape upon the floor. The sound of his breathing shifted, snorted, and then settled into the regular rhythm of a man deeply, finally, asleep.

Now was the time for me to act.

But, first, I had to get up.

This proved more difficult than I had expected. I had spent so long upon my knees, and my bones were so cold, that I could not raise either leg. In the end, I fell upon my side, letting out a muffled, "Oomph," as I landed. But that sound mingled with the breathing of the king and the snoring of the monk, and, after lying still for a while, I was sure that it had roused neither of them.

Then came the long and painful process of straightening out my body. Not even the prospect of the riches lavished upon the Book could hurry that, nor ease the pains that shot through leg and back and arm. I tried to time my stretching with Brother Odo, so that my gasps of pain would be masked by his snoring.

When I had finally got control of my body, I rolled on to my front and slowly pushed myself up to my feet.

The king hadn't stirred. Brother Odo was still snoring. The Danes might be arriving tomorrow. Sometimes, fortune veils the chances she throws before you behind a curtain of uncertainty: should I act now or should I wait for a better opportunity. But at other times, she reveals herself to you as flagrantly as any doxy desperate to earn some silver.

I went up to the altar, took the Book carefully from its stand, made my way quietly to the door and began to ease it open.

And sometimes, fortune reveals herself only to you to trick you.

Something slammed into the back of my head and, before I could say or do anything, I realised that I no longer had any command over my body. Very shortly afterwards, that realisation was followed by another: that I had no control over my mind. And then both realisations were lost in my sudden fall into the well of darkness.

Chapter 7

When I woke, my head felt as if it had been used for target practice during one of those long and tedious fighting games that the warriors of a king's household are wont to play. The sort of thing where a pig's bladder is blown up, tied to a stick and then they have to try and pierce it with thrown knives, while at the same time the other side have to avoid being struck in the eye by a flying knife. That's what my head felt like, only it did not split open each time a dagger of pain struck it — much though I wished it would. Instead, it tightened with each successive blow, in a manner that was all too authentic. On the one, and I fervently hope only, occasion when I have been stabbed by a blade, I remember thinking that it was odd. I would have expected a cutting or stabbing pain, but that is not what it felt like at all. Instead, it was like being hit by a club. And all because I didn't have the silver to pay her.

As some ability to think slowly returned — although as yet I could not move anything — I took some comfort in the thought that, since this was a cutting pain, I couldn't have been stabbed in the head. Nor did I feel the tale told by sticky liquid or, worse, the stretching of once sticky blood drying over the skin beneath. My blood, it seemed, was still where it belonged: inside me.

No, I must have hit my head. In the darkness, rushing to get out, I must have hit my head on the door lintel. In memory, I felt myself ducking in order to get into the church. That was it, that was what must have happened.

If I was fortunate, and had fallen outside, I might not even have woken Edmund. There was still time to carry out my plan.

All I had to do was move…

But nothing would move. It felt as if I had some sort of control over my limbs, but nothing happened when I tried to tell them to do something. I ventured, again, to open my eyes. On my first attempt, the light — no more than the first flush of dawn — had sent waves of pain crashing through my skull and I had as quickly closed them. But now I needed to see where I was and why I couldn't move. So, slowly, I crept my eyes open.

The first thing I saw was that I had fallen inside the church, not outside it. Then, I realised I must have staggered some distance before falling, for I saw that I was again somewhere near the altar. But it was not the base of the altar I saw, as I would if I were lying on my side, but the front of it.

I was sitting up.

How could I be sitting up if I had knocked myself out?

Then, I looked down, and saw that the reason I could move neither arms nor legs was that they were bound tight with rope, and I was sitting up because I was tied to one of the roof posts of the church.

"I am sorry."

I jerked my head round, then moaned at the pain flaring behind my eyes.

The king squatted down beside me and laid his hand upon my brow. "I am so very sorry."

"W-why am I tied up?"

"It is my fault, it is all my fault." Edmund sat back upon his heels and his eyes filled with tears. "You kept faith with me through the long watch, by your presence and your prayers strengthening me when my fears grew and my faith faltered and I would fain have got up and run from this place. But when you needed me to bolster your resolve, when in those lonely hours of the night the flesh weakened, I slept. As Peter and James and John slept in the garden, I slept when you needed me. Then the tempter came and called to you, in honey words whispering how you should take the Book to safety and preserve it from the defiling hands of pagans. It is no wonder and no shame that, faced with the temptation of the prince of this world, you yielded for a brief moment. I am sure you would quickly have regained your resolution but, by God's grace, I woke and saw you leaving with the Book, so I stopped you. And because I know that you would want me to ensure that you can never fall before this temptation again, I have bound you to this pillar." The king took my hand — or what he could find of my fingers under their covering of thick rope — and stroked it.

"We will not have to wait long. The Danes approach."

My head, which had still been muzzy from the after-effects of the blow it had taken, suddenly cleared. In one small corner of that dreadful clarity of thought, I missed the lost fog: safe there, I would have merely nodded vaguely at the king's words and laid my head back against the pillar to rest.

Instead, I cried, "What?" and threw myself against my bonds.

I might as well have tried to bowl over a boar. The king knew how to bind a man. The only thing I could move freely was my mouth, which I proceeded to move vigorously and coarsely until — "Mmph!" — I couldn't.

"I truly am sorry," said Edmund. "I would not have gagged you, but the Danes will soon be here, and I must be able to speak to them without interruption."

"Mmph, mmph!"

"Do not worry. I will remove the gag when the time comes so that you will have the chance to make your statement of faith. But first, you must let me speak with the Danes."

"Mmph, mmph, mmph!"

"Of course I will let you speak with them as well."

"Mmph."

"When the time comes for us to die as martyrs, in sacrifice for our people."

"Mmph, mmph, mmph, mmph!"

"I can see you are as eager to join the Lord in his kingdom as I am." Edmund leaned over and kissed my forehead, and I could see the tears of faith pooling in his eyes. My own eyes were swimming with tears too, but they were not the tears of faith. To think I should have got this far, and come so close to getting away with the Book, only for a lunatic king to truss me up and offer me to the Danes.

"Now I must go forth and meet the pagan king of this heathen army and offer him treasure greater than any he has ever known." Edmund stood up, murmuring prayers under his breath.

As the king made his way towards the door of the church, I looked round, searching for the only person who might be able to help me in my plight.

There he was. Brother Odo. And he wasn't tied up.

I waited for the sound of the door opening and closing, then started frantically nodding and shaking my head, as if I was having a fit.

Brother Odo came towards me and, as he came, I shook more.

Given my state of mind, it was not too difficult for me to look red and flushed, as if I was having difficulty breathing, and I gasped and gurgled to add to the effect.

"Brother Master," said Brother Odo, "the king gave me orders that I was not to free you."

I gasped and gurgled harder.

"Can you not breathe?"

I shook my head and began to roll my eyes.

"He did not say anything about the gag."

I nodded, but weakly, letting my eyes roll further back. Brother Odo reached down, undid the gag and released a flood of words.

"You've got to untie me, he's mad, we're all going to die! The Danes will take the Book, we'll die, untie me, I can't believe you let him tie me up like this… we'll die, come on, hurry up, what are you doing? Come on, we'll die, get these ropes off me, there's still time, we'll die…"

But Brother Odo shook his head and pointed down the nave of the church to the door.

I turned to look.

The door swung open.

Outside in the cold winter light was the king. But Edmund had been forced to his knees and a knife was being held across his throat. Behind him, holding him by the hair, was a thin whiplash of a man, wearing an iron crown and with an iron ring around his throat. He stared into the darkness within the church with narrowed eyes, but even from this distance I could see their coldness. There was no mercy in them, and no fear either.

Although I had never before seen him, I knew who held the king upon the edge of his knife: Ivarr, called by some the Boneless, eldest of the sons of Ragnarr and the one most feared. For while Ubba was more brutal and, tale told, strong enough to wrestle a bear to the ground, and Halfdan was the most feared axe man wherever the grey whale roads ran, Ivarr was subtle and far-seeing, knowing with all the skill of a fraudster where to find the fissures in a man's soul, and how to split them apart through the application of fear or greed.

"I hold the life of your king upon my knife."

Ivarr spoke our tongue as if he had heard it at his mother's breast. Men whispered, in the dark after the fires were banked down, that he had made a pact with the old gods, the ones our forefathers had worshipped, and that Woden One-Eye, the Deceiver, the Magician, had come to him and given him gifts of understanding and cunning, so that he might win back these lands for those thirsty old gods.

They were the sort of tales told when the wind moaned at the eaves of halls, and grey shapes moved amid the willow beds, and I had taken them as the stories to frighten the children to bed. But now, seeing Ivarr at the door, I began to believe them.

Ivarr gestured, and his companions, swords dully glittering, came cautiously into the church, eyes searching for hidden traps and hiding warriors.

What they found, was us.

They pulled Brother Odo roughly from the church and threw him to the ground in front of Ivarr. But me, they left in place, tied to the pillar, and took report of me to their king.

Ivarr came into the church.

I felt my bowels weaken as he approached. In desperation, I fixed my gaze upon the Book on the altar; I had already seen enough of the Dane to know that greeting him with my breeches stinking of my own excrement would not help my chances of living past this day.

Ivarr came into the church, but he kicked Edmund before him. Each time the king attempted to struggle to his feet, Ivarr kicked the knee from beneath him, sending him falling forwards again.

"This is it?" he asked, pointing at the altar.

Edmund began again to try to work his way to his feet. Ivarr kicked his knee once more, but this time I heard a crack, and Edmund fell sideways with a cry of pain.

"I did not tell you to stand," said Ivarr. "Is this it? The treasure you spoke of?"

The king rolled on to his side and looked up at the altar.

"It is a greater treasure than you know. It is life, and love, and truth, and an end to death."

"Really?" said Ivarr. "An end to death?" He pulled my head back and I felt the cold hard edge of his knife upon my throat. "So if I slit his throat, he will not die?"

Ivarr was not even looking at me, but at the king. I knew, if I was not to die in the next few moments, that I had to draw his attention to me.

"Gold," I said, "silver. Garnets. Rubies."

And Ivarr turned his hard cold gaze from the king to me.

"A man of understanding, not empty words. Yes, those are the treasures I seek. Where may I find them?"

"We put them in service to the treasure the king spoke of; we put them as cover and clothing to words."

"Words?" Then understanding flicked across Ivarr's face. He let go my hair and strode to the altar.

The Book stood open there, the words of the beginning of the fourth Gospel on display in the graceful hand of Abbot Maccus, the predecessor of Abbot Flory, who had written the words of the book through three years of labour and, having finished the writing of it, had made the greatest treasure of Medeshamstede. Then he had given the words into the hands of others, brothers Ulf, Mul and Eoppa, who bound and covered and decorated it, until the Book was as much a wonder when it lay closed upon the altar as when it was held open.

But Ivarr had no mind for written words — to him, they conveyed less than the tide marks on a beach. He reached out and closed the Book and, closing it, saw the gold and garnets of its cover and its hasps. The gold light shone on his face, the gold lust glowed in his eyes.

"Now *this* is treasure," he said. Then he turned back to me. "Treasure teller, why are you tied to a tree?"

"I tied him there," said Edmund. He reached to me and, using me as a support, began to once again, slowly, lever himself to his feet. For now, his gold lust assuaged, Ivarr saw no reason to kick him down once more.

Edmund stood, holding on to me.

"You asked for my submission, Ivarr, son of Ragnarr. Know this: never in this life will I submit to you unless you first swear oath and fealty to the Lord Christ. For our forefathers believed as you do, until they were brought news of life, and they forswore death and embraced this new life. Come, embrace it with me and I will embrace you as a brother and gladly call you lord, for we will all be retainers to the same lord."

Ivarr nodded slowly. "Very well."

Edmund cried out in joy, but Ivarr held up his hand.

"I said, very well. I will accept this god — once I have put him to the test. You say that he brings life? You say that he has defeated death? Then let us try this — let us try this on his servant." Ivarr gestured to his retainers. "Cut this man free," he said, pointing to me, "and put the king in his place."

They cut the ropes from me with quick strokes, then just as quickly tied Edmund to the pillar. They tied him with his back to the pillar, so he could see Ivarr and the other men gathered round him. From where they had thrown me, in the corner of the church, I could see Edmund's eyes scanning over the men ranged in front of him. His death stood there, among those men, and he looked for the face of the man who would kill him. For myself, I huddled deep in the shadows, hoping that I would be forgotten.

I wasn't.

Ivarr had his men pull me out of my hiding place. For a mercy, Thorgrim was not among the earls who had accompanied the sons of Ragnarr on this ride into the kingdom of the East Angles. I wondered if he would come, to join his king, and then, seeing me, denounce me. But that depended on me living long enough for his return from whatever task Ivarr had sent him upon.

As things were, it seemed unlikely that I would survive Ivarr's notice for Thorgrim to unmask me.

Pulled to where the king stood, Ivarr looked to me.

"I want you to watch," he said. "We will see how the king's god keeps oath: the king says he has been promised life. We will see if his god keeps his pledge for, if he does, I tell you here, with my men as witness, that I will put aside my gods and the gods of my forefathers and take this new god as my own. He has but to keep his pledge. Now, let us stand back and put this god to the test." Ivarr took a spear from one of his men and drove it, point first, into the hard packed ground at his feet. "Give me some more."

One after another, his men stuck their spears into the ground beside Ivarr, so that it looked as if he stood beside a clump of tall rushes.

"Who wants to go first?" Ivarr looked round his men. "You, Grimbald. You first."

A tall Dane stepped up beside Ivarr and pulled a spear free.

Edmund, tied to the pillar, turned to Ivarr.

"I give you warning, Ivarr, son of Ragnarr. Kill me this day and you will die before this year ends."

But Ivarr laughed. "Surely your god will preserve you? Do you begin to doubt?"

"The life he gives is eternal life, not life in this world."

"But life in this middle earth is what I want. Let's see if your god can give me more of that." And he turned and nodded to Grimbald.

The spear flew, its iron head glinting in the winter light streaming in through the door of the church, and pierced the king, striking him in the shoulder.

Ivarr laughed. "That was a terrible throw, Grimbald. He still lives! Maybe his god is protecting him."

"Give me leave to throw again, and he won't," said Grimbald.

But Ivarr shook his head.

"Let another have their turn." He gestured. "Olaf One Eye."

"One Eye!" protested Grimbald. "He's so blind he can't hit a door when he's standing in front of it."

"All the more reason to have him throw. I want to give the king's god every chance."

Olaf, who did indeed only have one eye and that rheumy, grasped and threw the spear in one movement.

It struck the king in the thigh and stuck there.

"A hit," cried Ivarr, turning to Edmund. "Your god is not keeping his promise very well."

But Edmund made no answer, although he yet lived. His eyes, I saw, were turned to the altar, where the Book still lay, and his lips moved silently.

"Another," cried Ivarr. "You, Erik."

Another spear flew.

"Magnus."

And another.

"Leif."

And another.

Edmund hung in his ropes, a man stippled with spears as if he was a human hedgehog. Blood covered his body, but yet he breathed.

"Oh, come on," said Ivarr. "Can't any of you kill him? All you've got to do is hit his heart."

"I would try once more," said Grimbald.

"If you don't manage to kill him this time," said Ivarr, "I'll have to do it myself. Otherwise I'll have to become a Christian!"

His men laughed at the joke, while Thorgrim took one of the two remaining spears. He hefted it, feeling its weight, then aimed and threw in a single motion. From where I was standing, I heard the rip of flesh and rasp of bone as the iron head plunged deep into Edmund's chest. The king slumped forward and the Northmen put up a cheer.

Only for the cry to die on their lips as the king slowly raised his head.

"Right," said Ivarr. "This has gone on long enough." He picked up the last remaining spear.

"R-remember your promise."

The words were blood bubbled and weak, but all there heard them in the silence of the church.

Ivarr hurled the spear with all his strength.

Edmund's body jerked back at its impact and did not fall forward again, for the spear had passed right through his body and pinned him to the pillar.

Ivarr stood long, staring at him, but the king did not move.

"Finally," he said, and turned away.

But as he did so, his men began to point and whisper, and some made warding gestures against the evil eye, and others clutched amulets and muttered charms of protection.

For Edmund raised his head and looked upon Ivarr and spoke.

"I live."

The son of Ragnarr stopped. I could see his face from where I stood and I saw there the clutch of fear men feel when the wraiths gather in the shadows outside the hall, or when the dead, unquiet, return to the living. But then Ivarr turned and, drawing his sword, swept it in an arc towards Edmund.

The stroke cut the king's head cleanly from his shoulders and it rolled away over the floor. The king's body slumped against the ropes that still held him up.

"You don't anymore," said Ivarr.

The head came to a rest near my feet and I looked with horror down at it to see the king's eyes searching, looking for their lost body, before rolling upwards to gaze on me before, finally, life left them.

Ivarr gestured at the head. "Take it outside, Grimbald, and throw it away." As Grimbald grabbed the king's hair and took the head out, Ivarr looked to me. "What am I going to do with you?"

"It's more a question of what *I* am going to do for *you*," I said. My life hung upon Ivarr's whim, but at least this was a contest of wit rather than swords; in such an arena, I had some chance.

"Really?" said Ivarr. "What can you do for me?"

"I have a riddle for you, Ivarr, and for your men, and on its answer lies the great and particular service I can do for you."

"Really?" Ivarr exchanged glances with some of his men. "This riddle sounds as if it would be better heard with food and drink, and somewhere warmer."

Which was how I found myself, an hour later, standing in what had been until recently King Edmund's great hall before Ivarr, and his two brothers, Halfdan and Ubba. They sat at the high table. In front of them, lying on the table, was the Book, while around the hall their men made short work of the supplies that the steward had left for us, while other retainers brought in a steady stream of barrels from the wagons slowly unloading outside the hall.

Brother Odo was sitting in a corner, trying to be invisible; the Danes only occasionally threw something at him, so he must have been largely successful. I, on the other hand, was for the moment the focus of the attentions of Ivarr, Halfdan and Ubba, along with the earls of the Great Army.

It was not where I wished to be.

"Come," said Ivarr, "let us hear this riddle before I decide what to do with you."

I made the courtesy to Ivarr and the two other sons of Ragnarr. "My lords, the riddle is straightforward, but on its answer lies your future. Answer truly, and your raven banner will always fly." I pointed at the long piece of cloth dangling from a spear that stood behind the brothers. It was the banner, stitched in the form of a raven, of the sons of Ragnarr and we had all heard the story told that the banner flew out when the sons were about to win a battle, but hung limp when they were about to lose.

It had been many years since the raven had not flown.

At my words, Ivarr looked to his brothers. "Shall we play, my brothers?"

Halfdan and Ubba exchanged glances, then both turned to look at me. With all three sons of Ragnarr staring at me, I felt as a hind must feel when it finds itself at bay and turns to see the hounds gathering for the kill. But everything depended on me giving no indication of the fear I felt in my bowels. In this, I was helped by a characteristic of mine. Most men, when struck by fear, flush or break into the fear sweat. While I too run cold, in me this shows by going pale, which men take for concentration or cold rage.

"What would you ask of us should you win this riddle contest?" asked Ubba. "Your life, I suppose?"

"No," I said, and I was gratified to see Ubba's eyes narrow in surprise. Even Ivarr leaned forward in interest. "No, should I win this contest, I would ask that I might give to you the answer to the riddle."

Ubba laughed, and turned to his brothers. "I say we let this contest begin. What say you?"

Halfdan nodded. "Yes. Ivarr?"

The eldest of the sons of Ragnarr looked long at me and I met his gaze, or at least appeared to. Even the bravest man would quail under Ivarr's cold gaze. But then, Ivarr also nodded.

"If we win, then your death shall be our pleasure, and that of our men," he said. At this, the men nearest to me roared in delight, and some began running the blades of their knives over the whetstones they carried in the pouch on their belts. "But if you win, then, yes, you may give us the answer to the riddle, so long as we should wish for it."

"Oh, you will," I said.

"Very well." Ivarr sat back, turning his knife to cleaning the dirt from under his fingernails. "Begin."

I nodded, my throat dry. But I must needs make myself heard through all the hall and before all the men within it, that the sons of Ragnarr be bound to their word.

"Hwæt!" So a scop calls a hall to listen; the skalds of the Danes utter a similar call. But now, I had to assert my difference. I was no Dane, and I was challenging them to the great and venerable riddle contest.

They must try to win so that I might win in turn.

Of course, if anyone guessed the answer to the riddle, then I would be giving long and painful entertainment to the men sharpening their knives.

"By the venerable rules of the riddle contest, let all here give witness that should I, Conrad, win the contest, then your kings shall allow me to give them the answer to the riddle. But should I lose the contest, then you will make sport of my dying for as long as your wit may prolong it."

"We kept a man alive near seven days once," said one of the men sitting near me. He looked me up and down. "I don't reckon you'd last more than three, but we'll see."

I affected a laugh. It was dry, but not too bad when discussing one's lingering death by torture with the man who would carry it out. "That's if you win." I scanned the man quickly. "Pigface."

The man spat his beer out in fury but the men around him fell about in laughter.

"How did you know his name is Hrolf the Hog?" one of them asked.

I pointed. "It wasn't that hard to guess." At that, Hrolf the Hog made for me, but the men around him, still laughing, hauled him back.

"If we win the contest, you'll get the first cut, Hrolf. Now let's hear the riddle."

With Hrolf held, and my audience ready, it was time to spring the riddle upon them.

"Here is the riddle: let all men hear. What is it that all kings desire yet no king ever asks for?"

I turned round, repeating the riddle so that everyone in the hall might hear what I said.

"What is it that all kings desire yet no king ever asks for?"

"Gold!"

The answer was yelled to accompanying laughter.

I held up my hand. "It is true that all kings desire gold, but I have heard that they ask for it too." I risked a glance at the high table. "How many pounds of gold did King Edmund give you to leave his kingdom, the first time you visited here?"

"More than you've ever seen!"

"No doubt, no doubt. But I say again: what is it that all kings desire yet no king ever asks for?"

"Hah, that is easy," said Ubba. "Victory."

"Again, it is true that all kings desire victory, but they all ask for it too. The kings of my people ask for it through the prayer of our priests and the kings of your people ask for it through the prayers of priests too — although the gods they pray to, men say, are different gods." I glanced at Ivarr as I spoke. He had not spoken yet, and I guessed he would not speak for a while, but his was the answer I feared. If any man in the hall might guess the answer to the riddle, it would be him.

But as I waited, in quiet dread, for Ivarr to speak, others essayed answers.

"Glory!"

"Honour!"

"Freya the Fair!" This last was accompanied by loud laughter.

I saw Halfdan look to his brother, and Ivarr's slight nod. He must think he had the answer.

"Wit," said Halfdan.

The hall went quiet.

"Good answer," I said. "But while it is true that no king asks for wit, only those kings with wits want more."

"Have you known a king without wit?" asked Ivarr, his voice quiet as steel.

I gestured around me. "You sit in his hall."

At that, even Ivarr smiled, while the men about him roared with laughter.

I looked to the watching hall, taking its mood. Now, they were ready for the answer. Only Ivarr, the eldest of Ragnarr's sons, remained to offer answer and the last chance to win the riddle contest.

"Would you answer, my lord?"

Ivarr watched me, silently, for a long minute. Then, sharply, he shook his head.

"Tell your answer, Conrad. I would hear it."

I nodded. My mouth felt suddenly dry. If my answer did not draw the soft sigh of recognition that accompanied a hall full of men nodding their heads that, yes, of course that was the right answer, then my life would be forfeit in the most unpleasant way these men could imagine — and their imaginations ran long in the inflicting of pain.

I licked my lips.

"What is it that all kings desire yet no king ever asks for?" I paused, feeling the motion as everyone in the hall sat closer to hear the answer.

"To be feared."

The long sigh came. I saw men nodding, turning to their neighbours, while others muttered, "Of course," sending the words in soft waves around the hall.

I heard all this but my eyes had never left the high table and the three sons of Ragnarr sitting there.

At the answer, Halfdan and Ubba nodded their approval. Only Ivarr remained blank, his iron eyes fixed upon me.

"You have won the contest," he said, "and we would have it of you." I felt my bowels relax, before they just as quickly tightened again. "But how will you grant to us this thing that all kings desire yet none ever ask for?"

"I will give it you with words," I said. "I will, by your leave, go before you into the last kingdom that still holds against you, the kingdom of Wessex, and tell the king there, and his thanes and his aldermen, the tale of the sons of Ragnarr and how they put our God and their gods to the test, and how their gods won. For once the men of Wessex lose the belief that God will protect them against you, for you are heathens, then they will quickly lose the will to fight you. For if God is not with us, then he must be with you; he must have made of you a scourge for our backs and a yoke for our necks, and they would as well fight the will of God as turn back the sun in the sky."

Ivarr looked cold iron at me.

"The king of the West Saxons is Æthelred. He is the fourth of his brothers to take the throne; the others have all died and there is but one other brother to rule after him, a weakling whom our spies tell us was destined for the church before his elders died. The West Saxons shall fall easily to us, Conrad. Why then should I let you go to them?"

"They will fall the more easily when they hear what I have to say."

Ivarr's iron eyes regarded me but he gave no answer.

"I will whisper fear into their ears and sow panic among their men, so that when they hear word that the Great Army marches upon their land, they will offer gold and silver, great weights of gold and silver, rather than take the field of slaughter against you. For I have seen your gods and our God put to the test, and I will tell what I saw."

Ivarr looked to his brothers. "What say you?"

Halfdan yawned. "He would make short sport."

Ubba was picking his teeth, but paused in the digging to look at me long enough that I might see the slow fire that glowed in his eyes. "He has wit enough to sow fear with his words. But has he wit enough to fear us though he be gone from our camp?"

"Oh, I have wit enough for that," I assured him. "I have looked upon the sons of Ragnarr and I know to fear them. I will spread that fear wherever I go, for it is the truth, and that makes the best tale."

"You think so?" said Ivarr. "The tales I hear are full of lies."

"But the best tales are mingled truth and lies, like the different colour threads that braid the edge of your tunic: unpick any thread, and the braid will fray."

"So what will you tell of truth, and what of lies, Conrad?"

"I will tell that which will give you best what all kings desire but do not ask for: to be feared."

Ivarr's gaze, mountain hard, fixed upon me. Then, finally, he nodded.

"Yes. You will leave on the morrow."

Chapter 8

The Danes feasted, but mostly drank, through the rest of the day and into the night. For my part, having received my life, I thought it best not to risk losing it at the hands of a drunken Northman searching for a fight, so I spent as much time as I could hunkered down in a corner of the hall, remaining as inconspicuous as possible. Ivarr had said I could leave on the morrow and I intended to live through to the next day.

But as the feast wound down into silence and snores, doubts began to assail me. What if Ivarr should change his mind? I would have no recourse. After all, I had no intention of really going to the kingdom of the West Saxons. Knowing, as I did, that it would be the next target for the Great Army, my plans, though ill formed, had at their centre one overriding idea: to stay as far away as possible from anywhere that the Great Army might be going. To that end, I had even thought of taking ship and crossing the Narrow Sea. There surely should be employment for a man of my talents at the court of Charles the Bald, king of the Franks. And if not there, then beyond, with the Emperor, Louis. I might even take myself to the other emperor in far Byzantium and see the wonders of the world on the way. The problem was that wonder walking was generally uncomfortable. It had taken me two months to recover from my youthful trip to Rome.

As sleep settled over the Danes, I unwound my creaking bones from the corner and went outside to relieve myself. The night was dark, without moon and only a few stars glittered through tears in the clouds. It was cold and still, the frost making star glitter on the ground, and even the Danish sentries nodded over their spears. To test them, I walked a short way out from the hall, into the dark to the shed where I had left the horse and donkey for my escape, and then returned, but none of the sentries challenged me.

The horse and donkey were indeed still in the shed, waiting patiently where I had left them. Should I wait upon Ivarr's permission for me to leave, or should I make my escape now?

The decision was made for me as I made to go back into the hall. For as I reached for the door, it opened. Brother Odo stood there, clutching something to his chest. He pointed to the object he held, then moved the cloth covering it slightly so that torchlight flickered upon garnet and gold.

He had taken the Book.

The sons of Ragnarr had left it upon the table in front of them throughout the feast, the great spoils of their taking of the kingdom of the East Angles. And now, Brother Odo had taken it back.

Of course, I could have dragged him back inside and put the Book back before anyone discovered it missing. Then I could have waited through the night for morning, and the hope that Ivarr would keep his word and let me go. I *could* have done these things, but I didn't.

Little Brother Odo had done what I would never have dared do, and stolen the Book from under the snout of the sleeping dragon. Now, we just had to get as far away as possible before the dragon woke.

Beside the door, the door warden snored, his breath rattling through his beard. I gestured Brother Odo to follow me and led him into the night, towards the shed where I had left the horse and donkey. For a moment I thought of trying to steal some better horses from the Danes, but just as quickly I decided against. Of all the guards, the men left in charge of the horses were the most likely to have stayed awake. The restlessness of their charges, and the danger of attack by wolves, meant that they would struggle to stay awake where the others had succumbed to the easy lure of sleep in a conquered kingdom.

No, we would have to make do with the beasts I had ready.

In the darkness of the shed, I risked whispered speech as we readied the beasts.

"How in middle earth did you get the Book away from the sons of Ragnarr?"

Brother Odo looked to me, his face a moon of surprise. "I took it," he said. "When I saw you creep out, I knew you must be getting ready to escape. I also knew, once you had got your escape ready, that you would return for the Book, so I decided I would get it ready for you."

"So, you just walked up to where it lay, in front of Ivarr and Ubba and Halfdan, and picked it up and walked out?"

"Yes," said Brother Odo. He looked suddenly stricken. "Did I do wrong?"

"No, no," I said. "It's just that not many men, including the bravest of warriors, would have risked taking such a treasure from under Ivarr's nose. Still, I suppose all you had to do was pick it up."

"Yes," said Brother Odo. "Well, after I'd moved his head."

"What?" I hissed.

"He was using it as a pillow. So I had to pick up his head and move it over. I kept on thinking he would wake up."

I swore. Brother Odo looked shocked but, for the moment, I did not care.

"We've got to get out of here; he will realise it's gone."

"I put something else there in place of the Book."

"What?" I asked as I turned my horse round and led him from the shed. Brother Odo followed with the donkey. Under Brother Odo's hands, it was proving surprisingly docile.

"A block of bread."

I nodded. That did almost make sense. The bread the steward had left behind had been so hard that it could easily be mistaken for a book. But still, it wouldn't mimic the jewels that crusted the book's binding.

"I pushed dry peas into the bread to make it seem like there were garnets embedded in it."

I looked at Brother Odo with something approaching respect. "We might just live to see the sun rise — but if we don't get a long way from here before the sun rises, we won't live to see it set again."

There were no guards in sight, so the temptation was to jump on to our mounts and ride away as quickly as possible. But if there was one sound that would wake a dozing sentry, it was the sound of galloping hooves. Although my bowels were telling me to get on the horse and ride, they would have to wait until we were a safe distance away.

So, with agonising slowness, we led our animals off along the path away from the king's hall. Only when the last faint gleam of the torches had disappeared did I decide it was safe to speed up.

"Get on the donkey," I said, as I mounted my horse. "Here, I'll take that," I added, reaching for the Book. It would be safe in my saddle bag — well, as safe as it could be, given that it was in my keeping.

But just as I was taking the Book from Brother Odo's slightly reluctant hands, I realised that we would have to speed up our escape drastically.

Although we were far enough away from the king's hall that the light from its torches were blocked by trees and bushes, it turned out we were still close enough to hear the sound of horns being sounded. Alarm horns.

The Danes had discovered we had gone. More to the point, they had discovered what we had taken when we left.

"We're going to die," I whispered.

"God has given us the Book," said Brother Odo, "he will not let the Danes catch us now."

I had considerably less confidence in God's reluctance to hand us over to the Danes for a slow and lingering death — after all, I had watched when he did nothing to save King Edmund — but at least Brother Odo's certainty helped me regain some presence of mind. There was no moon and the ground was ice hard — it would be difficult for them to find, let alone follow, our tracks in the dark. If we could move quietly, we could still get away. But which way? At the moment, we were following the trail we had taken on our way here, for I thought it least likely that the Great Army would go back the way it had come. However, now they would be searching for us, sending out scouts and search parties on the fastest horses they had, while all we had was one old horse and a stubborn donkey. We were not going to outrun them, so I would have to outthink them.

I had told Ivarr that I would go to Wessex and spread fear and panic there. But now, as Ivarr stood on the platform outside the king's great hall and decided in which direction to send his riders, he would look back on that conversation and think that I must have already planned to steal the Book and make my escape. Therefore, he would probably decide that Wessex was the place I was least likely to go. The quickest escape from Beodricesworth would be to ride to the River Lark, find a boat there and row down to where it joined the Ouse. Then the swift winter current would carry us to the Wash and passage on a sea going vessel to somewhere a long way from any Danes. *That* was the way Ivarr would send the first wave of riders.

When they returned, I hoped he would send scouts out on a general search, leaving the route west, towards Wessex, until last. So that was the way we would go.

Of course, in the chaos and confusion of waking up with a head sore from too much beer and too little sleep, even someone as cold minded as Ivarr might just issue a general order to all his men to find us, sending them scattering to the four quarters. Then, it would be only fortune that might save us from discovery and the long and excruciatingly painful death the Danes would devise for us. In the normal course of events, I could not imagine ever pleading for death, but having once come across the remains of some men the Danes had had sport with, I thought I might save them the bother: if I saw I was about to be taken, I would do the deed myself.

Then again, I probably wouldn't. Self slaughter was not in my nature.

"We'll go west, head for the Old Road," I told Brother Odo, who was still looking with wide and fearful eyes back in the direction of the king's hall and the tumult erupting from it. "But we'll go across country until we strike it," I added, turning my beast off the path and, near as I could judge, heading west.

It's no easy matter heading in any direction on a dark night when the clouds make sport with the Plough, sometimes revealing it but more often hiding it. Whenever the Plough did appear, I would try to take a bearing on some darker shadow on the horizon and steer us towards that. We were at least fortunate in that the country we were crossing was broken up by copses and small woods, and though some of it had been ploughed the ploughmen must have rushed their oxen for the furrows were shallow and easy for my horse to step over. Brother Odo's donkey found them rather harder going, but with Brother Odo on its back, it trudged on with the minimum amount of protest you could expect from a donkey.

So we made our way quietly through the dark of the night, listening always for the sound of pursuit. But the sounds had died away as we went and, as the first lightening of dawn began to warm the sky behind us, I dared to think that we would live through the night.

We had gone in near silence, our breath riding with us and mingling with the breath of the horse and donkey. The only sound had been the quiet murmurs of Brother Odo encouraging his donkey to keep going — he had apparently named the beast Buttercup, for some unfathomable reason, as the scrofulous beast was to my eye as far from a little yellow flower as it was possible to get while remaining a living creature. I was thankful that my horse appeared to need no such coddling, although I named it Wolfbait as promise of what would happen to the beast if it went lame on me. The horse appeared to pay no heed to its new name but kept plodding stolidly on. Indeed, such was its stolidity that I had to haul its head virtually back to my own before it realised I was telling it to stop.

In the grey of the pre-dawn light I could see a trail ahead, cutting across the way we were heading, its path marked white by the chalk that feet and hooves had exposed beneath the surface layer of soil and grass.

We had come to the Old Road, that some named the Icknield Way. It rose in the far south east of the country, from the town of Exanceaster, then made its way west via the high chalk ridges of the hills and downland until it ended on the shore of the grey sea in the land of the East Angles. Some say it was first made by giants, their great feet wearing away the flesh of the land to reveal the bones beneath, but then, you'll always find someone who'll say whatever it is you're looking at was made by giants. For myself, I think the Old Road was made by the feet of the old people, the ones who lived in this land before the emperors came from over the sea, and the hooves of their sheep and goats and cattle.

As we turned onto the Old Road, having first looked carefully to see that there was no one else riding it, I soon realised that those people who made the road by their tramping had had the good sense to walk the dry ridges from which the winter rains drained quickly. My horse walked almost dry shod and, with the ground firm beneath his hooves, he plodded along with something approaching confidence. With the sun now lurking below the horizon and the land coming to light around us, I decided that we could risk picking up the pace. In the daylight, the Danes would speed up their own search, so we needed to put as much distance between them and us as possible.

I turned back to Brother Odo. "Keep up," I said, then urged my horse into a canter. Wolfbait was not at all pleased at this turn of events, and only by constantly heeling his flanks could I get him to maintain the pace. Indeed, I had to put so much effort into kicking him that my legs began to ache.

So poor was the pace Wolfbait was setting that Brother Odo and Buttercup had little difficulty keeping up. When I saw a shadowed copse of alder and poplar in a dell by the track, I gestured for them to follow me and I rode Wolfbait down into the trees.

"It is good of you to give the animals a chance to rest," Brother Odo said as he climbed down off the donkey.

"We can't afford to have either of them go lame on us," I said. "But this is not a chance for them to rest, but for us to eat." I opened the saddle bags and handed out bread and hard cheese. I had had the wit to equip Wolfbait and Buttercup with provisions when I had left them ready for my escape in the shed.

As we ate, I looked, from the shelter of the trees, at the line of the track. To the west, the direction in which we were going, it ran steadily along ridge tops and, so far as I could see, there were no riders upon it. But the way back east was not so clear. The path wound, concealing itself, and I could not see far. Riders might be approaching and we would only know when they were almost upon us. We would do better to keep on.

I pointed west. "You have good eyes, Brother Odo. There, what do you see?"

Brother Odo looked to the west, squinting his eyes then opening them wide.

"I see the road running west but where it comes to the edge of sight, there I think I see houses, a village maybe, and the signs of another way heading from south to north."

I nodded. "That will be where the road built by the emperors of old, called Ermine Street, crosses the Old Road. There is a village there, a mean place of little wealth called Rohesia's Cross. But as it lies at the crossing of the ways, we should be able to buy fresh mounts there." I patted Wolfbait's neck. "I should think they'll use you for dog meat."

"I should like to keep Buttercup," said Brother Odo. "He is a true and faithful beast."

I climbed up on to my reluctant mount. Wolfbait gave every indication of thinking his break insufficient. "You're welcome to him, though I wouldn't want to be riding a donkey if the Danes catch up with us. Me, I'm going to find a better ride."

"What have you called your horse?" asked Brother Odo as he trotted after me.

"Wolfbait."

"No!" he said, stopping his animal's ears. "Don't listen, Buttercup."

"Tell Buttercup he'll be wolfbait too, unless he picks his hooves up." With that, I urged my horse into a trot. Or at least, I attempted to. The effect was rather ruined by my having to hack away with my heels at the beast's unresponsive flanks, like a wife beating the dust from her blankets. Wolfbait eventually stumbled into a trot — more as a result of my leaning forward and whispering into his ears that I would hamstring him and leave him for the wolves rather than in response to my frantic kicking — and we made good progress along the Old Road towards Rohesia's Cross. "Can you see the cross?" I asked Brother Odo as we neared the scattering of dwellings that marked the crossroads.

"Er, no," he said. "But I can see some riders on the road behind us."

Chapter 9

I turned round. From this distance, I could not tell how many — but there were enough.

This, I thought, *is what I get for carelessness*. I thought I had got away with life and Book and had let down my guard. Now the Danes were going to catch me and kill me… slowly.

For once, Wolfbait did what I asked him: he began to gallop frantically towards Rohesia's Cross. If we could get in among the houses, there was a chance I might be able to hide, particularly as this was a settlement the Danes had not yet sacked. If fortune was with me, the Danes would get distracted by some fleeing girl or hastily hidden treasure. But all that depended on me getting to the village before they did and, looking back, I could see the riders were gaining on us quickly.

"Brother Odo, I'll get the Book to safety, slow them down."

"How?" he wailed after me, but I was already galloping away from him. It would take the Danes a precious few moments to take Brother Odo captive or to kill him — I didn't much mind which, so long as it took them some time. It was just a pity he wasn't a warrior, then he could have bought me minutes rather than a few heartbeats.

I looked over my shoulder to see how he was doing, only to see

EDOARDO ALBERT

Brother Odo riding after me as fast as the pursuit.

"Go back!" I yelled. "Stop them!"

"I'm trying," Brother Odo cried, and indeed I could see he was hauling on the bridle. "Buttercup won't let me!"

The donkey had his ears pinned back and his head pushed forward. Great gobbets of froth fell from the sides of his mouth where he chewed the bit, but he would not stop, despite Brother Odo's frantic hauling at the bridle. It seemed that the beast was not going to allow Brother Odo to sacrifice himself on my behalf.

If I lived, I would have to see to that animal.

But at the moment, the prospects did not seem good.

The villagers, seeing our frantic approach, were sounding the alarm: bells and cries and whistles signified a general flight. People were running out into the fields, trying to get into the relative safety of the surrounding woods before the Danes arrived. Some ran with nothing but their clothes — one man, caught short, was running bare-bottomed for cover — but others struggled under hastily-grabbed treasures, from babes in arms to ancient shields and swords that, from the look of them, were last wielded by the soldiers of the emperors of old. Even the halt and the lame hobbled away, being helped, carried and sometimes simply dragged towards cover.

I thought of riding after them and trying to find cover myself among the trees, and would have done so but for Wolfbait slowing down. Despite my frantic kicking, and even with the shouts of the pursuing Danes beginning to reach us, he could not speed up: the beast was shot.

My only chance lay in getting in among the houses. At least there the Danes would no longer be able to see me and I might be able to find somewhere to hide, or a line of escape not visible to them. Risking a look back — a risk both because I might fall off and because seeing the pursuit might send me into such a funk of fear that I would be unable to do anything — I saw that there were fewer men chasing us than I had feared. Only five or six. The odds were still unfavourable — for my part, I would only fight the Danes if the odds were four to one in my favour and I could hide at the back — but at least that meant they could not put up sentries all around Rohesia's Cross and then search it house by house.

What I needed to do was slow them down.

If Buttercup wouldn't let Brother Odo act as my rearguard, there was, I realised, another way of drawing their attention away from me. But could I live with myself afterwards, if I did this to survive?

With Wolfbait all but blown and slowing down, I drew the Book from my saddlebag. The golden hasp that sealed it, and the golden clamps that bound it felt cool and innocent under my touch, like a willing young girl.

The Book was undefiled.

Yes, I could live with myself perfectly well if I did this.

I glanced back again. The Danes were still some distance behind, but with Wolfbait blown there was no chance of outrunning them. I would have to distract them.

Time to deflower the Book.

Gripping Wolfbait with my knees, I grasped the golden hasp and tried to twist it off. But the metal slipped under my fingers, slick with fear sweat, and the garnets slid from my grasp. It was like trying to grab a fish.

I would have to cut it off. But that would be impossible on Wolfbait; the knife would likely slide off and stick me in the stomach.

I was almost in among the houses now. Seeing a jumble of huts and sheds and workshops behind one of the larger houses in the village, I pulled Wolfbait in among the buildings and slid off his back. Now we were out of sight of the pursuing Danes for a few precious minutes.

Brother Odo, following on Buttercup, pulled the donkey into the same space, nearly crashing into a shed as he did so and sending a pile of timber staves tumbling to the ground. When in fear of my life, I find my mind becomes heightened and aware of things that it might otherwise miss. Even as I was drawing my knife and starting to prise the hasp from the Book I remember thinking it was strange to see mining staves in Rohesia's Cross, since we were far from any mines that I knew of.

"What are you doing?" Brother Odo asked, staring at me in wide-mouthed horror.

"Buying us some time," I said. Damn this Book. It was so well made that even with a knife I was having to saw away at the bindings that tied the hasp to the cover.

"B-but Brother Master, we must defend the Book, not defile it," said Brother Odo.

"I'm only giving them part of it," I said. "Now come on, give me a hand."

"No, Brother Master, no!"

I looked up to see actual tears in Brother Odo's eyes, he was so upset at what I was doing.

"You put your soul in peril, Brother Master, please, please stop."

I continued frantically sawing, making precious little progress. So, it wasn't so much the Book he was concerned about but my soul. Well, little did he know about the general state of that.

"Brother Master, please, don't do this." The tears were now running down his cheeks. He held his arms out to me imploringly. "Devils will drag you down to Hell, Brother Master, please stop."

I needed more leverage to get the hasp off. Looking round, I saw a saw horse and, putting the book on it, I began to pry the hasp away from the cover.

"They will take you to…to…" Brother Odo was so upset he couldn't even finish what he was saying. Just as well; there wasn't much time before the Danes would be on us and I had to leave the hasp out as distraction, find myself somewhere to hide and send Brother Odo out as a decoy before they arrived.

But there was a quality about his silence that made me look up. He wasn't talking anymore because he was pointing, pointing at the ground at my feet, and the look on his face was one that, once seen, could never be forgotten.

I have seen fear on men's faces many times and, if I had a glass to hand I'd have seen it on my own face much more often, but in all those cases it was the simple fear of death and its accompanying pains that filled the faces I was looking at. This, the look on Brother Odo's face, was something different. This was a fear greater than the fear of death, or pain, or loss. This was the fear of an eternity of punishment. This was the fear of Hell, risen.

"T-the Devil has come," said Brother Odo, pointing, and I looked and saw two hands, twisted and gnarled and seamed red, reaching for my ankles from a great hole that had suddenly opened up in the ground behind me. The hole had not been there before. Neither had the hands.

Before I could move, or do anything, the hands gripped my ankles and tugged me down, screaming, into the hole, my chin bouncing on its edge so that my eyes blurred. The last thing I saw clearly was Brother Odo turning, his mouth open in a scream of terror, as he ran from me and the demon dragging me down to Hell. As my vision blurred over and I fell, I heard his voice trailing into the distance, screaming, "The Devil, the Devil, the Devil has risen from Hell, run, run, run!"

Chapter 10

I woke in Hell.

I closed my eyes. At least, even though I was dead, I could still do that.

This, I decided, was completely unfair. My plan all along had been to enjoy the pleasures of this world and then, when the time came, to make a deathbed confession so that I could enter into the rather vague joys of Heaven. When I'd asked Abbot Flory what was so good about spending eternity with God, he'd looked first shocked and then unsure, before mumbling something about the beatific vision and sending me back to the abbey church to do double duty of prayer. So far as I could see, the beatific vision meant spending forever staring at God. Now, if God was a beautiful woman with little in the way of clothing, I could imagine myself spending a good few years staring, but since I knew what God looked like — bearded and pierced — I really couldn't see how I was going to spend eternity staring at him and calling it beatific. Boring at best, and quite possibly horrific. Still, it was better than the alternative: some people might like being whipped and tortured and burned, but I'm not one of them. So I had decided that I would spend my lifetime indulging in the definite pleasures of the flesh and then confess on my deathbed, enter an immediate state of grace, and go straight to Heaven without passing Hell. It all sounded so easy, I did wonder why God hadn't spotted the loophole.

As it turned out, he had.

I was dead and I'd died without even knowing it and now I was in Hell.

My head was aching, my limbs were sore and my eyes hurt even when closed. I shifted slightly and some of my pains eased.

That was a relief. From what I'd been told there was no ease to the pains of Hell.

I tried opening my eyes again. Hell was smaller than I had expected.

It appeared to be a dark chamber, lit by a torch. I was lying on my side with my back against a wall, and the further wall gradually became visible as my sight cleared. It was only fifteen, maybe twenty feet away. Looking upwards — my head still hurt too much to move it, so I looked with my eyes — the ceiling, which was shaped like a bell, was higher. Maybe twenty-five feet above me.

The walls, white like bone, were incised with strange carvings and in front of some of them candles burned on sconces, sending flickering shadows over the images behind them. At first I thought the images were demons and devils, but as my sight cleared and the throbbing in my head reduced, I became less sure. They could be demons, but a lot of them looked like people, although people with strange, curved limbs and distorted heads.

My mouth was dry and I tried to lick my lips. I couldn't. I was gagged. Cloth filled my mouth and, when I tried to remove it, I realised my hands were tied as well. So, the tortures of Hell were soon to start.

"You're awake."

I looked round — an authentically hellish pain stabbed through my head when I moved it, which would have made me whimper if my mouth had not been stuffed with cloth — and I saw a demon, squatting on its haunches, staring at me with red eyes. I knew it was a demon because its skin was chalk white, the white of the drowned dragged from the sea, and its body veined red.

But the demon did not seem to have horns, nor tail, nor the hooved feet I had expected. It was also rather smaller than I had anticipated. I had expected the princes of Hell to be great towering figures of smoke and shadow and fire. This was a small, hunkering creature that reminded me more of a frog than anything else.

I answered with the best mumble I could manage, given the gag.

"If I take off the gag, you must promise not to scream." The demon pointed upwards. "They might hear you."

I nodded.

"You promise?"

I nodded again, more vigorously.

The demon crept to me on hands and knees. Its fingers felt hot and dusty on my skin. And when it leaned over me, I heard the rattle of wheezy breath and then a cough hacked at its body.

If this was a demon, it seemed to be in markedly poor health.

I was beginning to suspect that I was not dead after all. But then, where was I? The last thing I remembered were the hands, reaching up from the ground to drag me down into what I had reasonably supposed was Hell.

"You're not a demon, are you?" I asked the demon when it had removed the gag from my mouth.

The demon shook its head, and clouds of white dust flew from its hair. "No, I'm not a demon," he said. "I am doing God's bidding."

"What has he bid you do?" I asked.

"Dig this," he said, and his gesture took in the cave around us.

I looked round again at the space I was in. If God had told my captor to dig it, I was mystified as to the reason.

"What is it?" I asked.

"A sanctuary," said the man. "An ark underground."

"Might be a little small?" I ventured. "Or are you planning to extend it?"

"Hah!" the man cackled. "It is not that sort of ark. It is the ark for the covenant that the Lord will enter into with His people in this land — there, can you not see the pictures, telling the glory He plans for us?" He gestured to take in the crude carvings scored into the walls of the cavern, some of which were daubed with paint.

Working on the basis that a man who has tied me up is not looking for honest criticism, I said, "They're marvellous." When his face did not brighten, I added, "Unique."

That worked. The man smiled, the shy smile of a man who hopes for praise but rarely receives it — in this case, probably because he was hidden underground engaged on a completely mad project.

"You are right." He sat back on his heels and stared at me. It was a look of appraisal that reminded me all too much of the calculating stares of the slave traders who had bought the monks of Medeshamstede. "It was not me that told you this, but God. He has infused you with knowledge and insight." The little man broke into a relieved smile. "He has sent you to me to help me in my task."

"Oh, yes, I'm sure He has," I said. "But if I'm to help you, I will really need to be released from these bonds."

But the little man shook his head. "You will aid me in prayer and counsel first. Only when you have proved yourself as much to my wit as to my heart will I release you from your bonds, so that you may join me in carving the covenant upon these walls."

"How long do you anticipate me joining you in prayer and counsel before I get the chance to do some carving too?" I asked. "For God has already put in my heart the images I will make."

"Not long," he said. "Two or three years."

"Two or three *years*… Er, are those years in the eyes of God or the eyes of man?"

"Oh, years in the eyes of man. I would not want to discourage you."

"Not in the slightest." I tried to look modestly eager. "It is only that I fear that, by then, God will have placed so many pictures in my heart that there will not be space left here to carve them."

"Then we will make it bigger." The little man gestured round at the lamp-lit space around us. "This has taken me forty-eight years to dig; forty-eight years of solitude and silence. Now, at last, I have someone to share my work with."

I stared at the little man.

"Do you mean that no one else knows of this place?"

He shook his head. "No one."

"But what of the people of Rohesia's Cross? You're not telling me that none of them know of what you have done here?"

He shook his head again. "No."

"But how could you keep this place secret?"

"The common people of the village fear me. Before I was called, I was their blacksmith…" he looked down at his withered arms and legs and shook his head, "though by my flesh you might not think so. For the work has leeched the flesh from my bones, leaving me whitened for death before my time. The men of Rohesia's Cross leave me, passing me by as one already dead. Besides, I do God's work in darkness, digging through the night and taking the spoil before dawn to lay it out in the fields — the people, seeing my white leavings, whisper that it is the work of elves and wights, and keep all the further from me."

I nodded. "God has set you apart. Now He has sent me to join you, and I will join your work in prayer and counsel for however long it takes before I may add my pictures to yours and we make the covenant of the Lord."

The little man nodded, apparently relieved that I had agreed to join him. Even in his solitude, he realised that although God might make a promise, men would often obstruct its fulfilment. That I had agreed so easily told him that his mission was true and his vision clear.

"But I do have one question. How did the Danes not see where you had taken me?"

"Ah, that is where God has shown me his mercy. He revealed this cave to me, although I have since much enlarged it, when the floor of my smithy fell out beneath me and I descended into the earth below. At first, I thought that for my sins, the devil himself had dragged me down into Hell, but when I realised that I was alone, in a cave, God's great plan began to reveal itself to me. And when I realised that no other men in Rohesia's Cross knew of this place, everything slowly became clear. The entrance is concealed, yet from it I might observe that which happens in the village. That is how I saw you and God spoke in my heart, telling me to claim you for my work."

"For my part, I am glad you did, for the Danes were about to claim me for *their* work — and that is no work I would be doing." I looked round. "Speaking of work, I was doing God's work when you grabbed me, seeking to save the Holy Book from the depredations of the Danes, who would profane its scriptures and strip it of the decoration by which we have sought to give glory to God." I paused. "I don't suppose you saw the Book when you dragged me down into your cavern?"

The little man smiled. "In truth, it was by the Book I saw in your hands that I knew in my heart that you are a man of God, beloved of the Spirit, and one worthy to aid me in my labours. For when the work here is done, we shall set the Book in a niche in our cave of the covenant, and each shall give the other glory."

"So, you have it then? The Book?"

"Oh, yes. Here." And the little man pulled back the pile of sacking in one corner to reveal the Book.

Everything was suddenly looking much better. From certain death at the hands of the Danes, through eternal damnation in Hell, I now found myself with the Book — *my* Book as I thought of it — still within reach, the Danes presumably gone and Hell postponed for the present. All I had to do was get free of my bonds, get hold of the Book, and get away from my mad captor. How hard was that going to be?

It proved somewhat harder than I had hoped.

I had expected to be free in a few hours, but Gotho, my captor, proved to be more cautious than I had anticipated. The entrance to the cave was by the way I'd come in: up to the roof by a rickety ladder and then a climb up a vertical tunnel to the world outside. But the ropes Gotho had tied me with were tight and had almost no give. As soon as he went out to see if the Danes had gone, I set to working on the knots, alternately tightening and loosening them, attempting to work some slack into the ropes. But in the hour he was gone, I had not managed to loosen them at all. Luckily, I heard his return, scrabbling down what sounded to be a tight tunnel, so I feigned a tranquil acceptance of my fate and awaited his arrival with the sort of beatific expression that young monks feigned when they wanted to impress the abbot with their piety and thus be spared the task of mucking out the pigs.

It worked better with Gotho than with Abbot Flory — who always ascribed such expressions to constipation rather than exaltation of the spirit, invariably putting the novice on a diet of bowel-loosening food and labour. Gotho, seeing my lips moving and my eyes upraised — I was actually engaged in trying to count just how many pictures my captor had inscribed into the cavern — raised his own hands and joined me in praise and worship, falling to his knees beside my prone body.

"Would the praise not be greater if I might join you on my knees?" I asked Gotho, after a suitable period of mumbling on my part, interspersed with impressive-sounding Latin phrases.

"Indeed it will," said Gotho. "When the time comes."

"All things in time," I said, returning to my mumbling, interspersed with which were some murmured Latin curses.

So matters continued through the next day. Gotho fed me some foul porridge and gave me to drink of worse ale. According to his account, the Danes still lingered in the area around Rohesia's Cross, although they did not make camp in the village itself but stayed without the hedge and fences that marked the village's boundaries.

So matters might have continued for a third day — which might have been apt, but I had business to attend to more urgent than the harrowing of hell — had my belly not begun to gripe me on the afternoon of that second day. Not that I had knowledge of whether it was day or night in the hole to which I had been consigned, but so Gotho told me it was. On this afternoon, my bowels tightened and the most fearful aching gripped my insides, as if the demons I'd feared when I first woke in this pit were now digging their claws into my guts.

I affected forbearance in the face of pain, making only the slightest whimper when the gripe struck, but such was the intensity of my suffering that Gotho soon saw my ill. When he asked, I waved it away, the first and second time. But on the third, in trying to say I was well, I let a hiss of pain through my teeth, and then when he asked again, admitted that the gripes had seized my belly.

"I — I will try to hold it in," I said. "B-but it may be beyond me. I would fain not foul this holy place with the foulness of my bowels but I fear I may not long endure." To drive home my point, I let loose the fart that I had carefully built up in my bowels. The only food I'd had the past two days was Gotho's porridge and the fart gave testament to my sole sustenance.

Gotho dragged me upright. "I know you are a man of truth, but my soul tells me I must do as God commanded, and keep you bound for two years before freeing you. But I will not have this place befouled by your noxious excretions." Gotho got behind me and, grabbing hold under my arms, began to pull. "I will take you forth."

"Wh-what about the Danes?"

"They have gone," said Gotho, dragging me to the ladder, my heels scoring lines on the chalk floor.

I am not the heaviest of men, though not the lightest either, and on that journey I made myself as heavy as ever a man has been: catching my feet on whatever obstruction I could find, hanging as inert as lead in Gotho's grasp. I struggled by my inaction to make him work harder than he had ever worked before. By the puffs, grunts and oaths Gotho was uttering, and the way his fingers were sweating up and slipping from their grasp, I was succeeding. Finally, he stopped, panting.

I let loose another fart and groaned. "I can't hold it much longer."

"I-if I unbind your legs, you will swear not to run?" he asked.

My bowels griped again. "I won't be running anywhere, Gotho: I'll be squatting. But if you don't let me loose soon, you'll be cleaning out my breeches."

"All right." Gotho took out his knife and sawed through the ropes holding my legs, then helped me up. "Quick," he said.

"I'm trying," I said. Legs that had been held immobile for the past two days struggled to hold me upright and get me moving despite the most urgent promptings. Another fart trumpeted from my bottom. I really could not hold out much longer.

"Come on," said Gotho, grabbing my still-bound arms and, going before me, he began to help me up the ladder.

Climbing even a sturdy ladder without the use of arms is no easy task: the ladder Gotho had made to the ceiling was not sturdy and even with him holding me from above, I nearly fell off a couple of times before I got to the ceiling. But once in the tunnel, the climb became easier, since the narrow space held me firm, while my feet found the metal rungs Gotho had driven into the side of the tunnel without too much searching.

I came to the entrance to the cavern. It was narrow, barely wide enough for head and shoulders to pass through. Gotho pushed it open. The sudden inrush of light all but blinded me and, if the tunnel had not been so tight about my shoulders, I would have fallen back down into the cavern beneath.

Even without use of my hands I was up after Gotho as if I had a fire up my bottom — for I did.

Emerging into the open air, a few things happened almost together. I was struck by the bitterness of the wind, cutting across the bare winter land from the east. Then I realised that all the plans I had hatched for turning bowel gripes into my longed-for escape were about to become nothing more than futile imaginings. For as I clambered up into the day my long repressed bowels announced that they would brook no further delay. No, not for a single moment longer.

"Pull my breeches down," I roared at Gotho. "I'm going to shit myself!"

Which was when more things happened almost together.

133

Gotho grabbed my breeches and pulled them down, I bent over and my bowels finally let go.

Or not so much let go as *exploded*.

Their contents flew out of me in a stinking jet. I think, if there had been nothing blocking the way, my all-too-liquid stool might have gushed ten feet or more. Unfortunately for Gotho, there was something in the way — and he was it.

Such was my relief that I did not hear his strangled, choking cries. I was enjoying the blessed, stinking relief. Only when the last of the accumulated contents of my bowels had been evacuated in a final convulsive heave did I begin to hear the strangled sounds from behind me.

I looked round to see Gotho lying on the ground; only, I did not recognise him as Gotho. The creature of chalk and dust had gone. Behind me was a man of dirty, dripping brown. Only his eyes, when he opened them, were white. He stared at me, not saying anything.

"You'd better go and wash yourself," I said.

Dumbly, Gotho nodded, got to his feet and stumbled off. From the way he crashed into things, it seemed that he could not see where he was going.

As for me, I was suddenly alone and above ground, unbound from the waist down, and contentedly, completely relieved.

Freeing my hands was straightforward. There had been little enough to Rohesia's Cross — at least above ground — before the Danes had visited. There was now even less, and much of it was jagged in some way. I sawed the ropes through on a shard of metal, sticking from a door post, cleaned my bottom with water and hay, pulled up my breeches and, taking a deep breath, did something I would not have done for any whore in Christendom: I went back underground. But if not even the finest whore in Christendom could have called me into the cavern, the Book could.

Less than a minute later, I came back to the light. There was no sign of Gotho, but it would take more than a few minutes for him to wash himself clean from what he was covered with. Now, if only the Danes had somehow missed Wolfbait, I would make my escape.

I began casting quickly back and forth through the ruins of Rohesia's Cross, looking between the burned out buildings and torn down huts, until I turned a corner to a sight much less helpful to my swift escape.

"Odo!"

Chapter 11

Brother Odo lifted his head. The lifting of it was long, painful and slow, for he was hanging from a tree. The Danes had crucified him.

"B-brother Master," he gasped. "I prayed to God to take me and release you from Hell."

I do not pretend to be a good man. I confess that my first thought on seeing Brother Odo hanging from the tree was to consider how much he would slow me if I should take him down from the tree, swiftly followed by the inclination to leave him where he was (after all, if the Danes returned and found him gone they might suspect that I had come back to get him and resume their search for me). Whenever Abbot Flory told us the parable of the Good Samaritan, my sympathy always lay with the men who passed by on the other side. Who would want to be landed with a beaten up victim of brigands with no money to pay for his care? Indeed, I had closed my face and started to turn away when Brother Odo said something that made me stop, turn back and help him, reasonably gently, down from the tree.

"Wolfbait."

"You know where he is?"

But his head had slumped on to his chest, his eyes closed, and I had no choice but to cut him down. At least the Danes had used ropes rather than nails to tie him to the tree, although judging from the bruises and cuts on his body (they'd stripped him down to his breeches), they'd treated him hard beforehand. Looking at the way his flesh had mottled blue under the wind, the winter lash must have done as much harm as the Danes. He would be fortunate to retain all his fingers and toes.

I looked around, searching for some sign of Gotho, but at least there was no sight of him. He would need a swift flowing stream to wash himself and, if my lady fortune favoured me, he would die from the chill of the winter water. Nor was there any sign of the Danes. But if there was no sign of the Danes, nor was there any trace of the residents of Rohesia's Cross: those who had escaped being taken as slaves must still be hiding in the woods and copses.

I could not stay here, with or without Brother Odo. But I also had the Book. I could not carry both monk and Book. Naturally, if it came to a choice, I would leave Brother Odo, but if he knew where to find Wolfbait, then it would be worth my while getting him to talk.

It would all be a lot easier if Brother Odo just woke up and told me where to find Wolfbait — even Buttercup would be useful.

I slapped Brother Odo's unresponsive face.

"Do you know where Wolfbait is?"

It was for his own good. If I couldn't find the beasts, then I'd have to leave Brother Odo. So I slapped him again, trying to beat his wits back into him and, for a surety, his eyes opened, staring and wide, and he reached up and grasped me convulsively.

"B-brother Master? It is you?"

"Yes, yes, it's me. Where's Wolfbait?"

Brother Odo shook his head, the wits slowly leaking from his eyes. I slapped them back in again.

"My horse. Or the donkey. We've got to find them."

"B-Buttercup?"

"Yes, Buttercup. Where is he?"

Brother Odo pursed his cracked lips and made a hissing noise. He tried again, but the hissing just got louder.

"What are you trying to do?"

Brother Odo made no answer in words, but tried once more, his frustration at his failures plain from the upset on his face. This time, the wind through his lips blew into a whistle, a faltering but rising note.

Almost at once, the whistle was answered by the swift clop of approaching hooves. Turning, I saw the long, mournful face of Brother Odo's donkey, Buttercup, making faster pace than I'd ever seen it do before, and behind it, as if following, my own beast, Wolfbait.

How they'd escaped the Danes I could not imagine — but then, I had no idea how Brother Odo had managed to survive the encounter, either.

In the end, it was curiosity that led me to push the semi-conscious monk up on to the donkey: the only way of finding out how he had survived and kept the beasts with him was to take him with me. So I set off on Wolfbait with Buttercup following behind with all the care of a mother carrying her first born. Whenever Brother Odo started to sway, Buttercup would turn its head and bray him back into the saddle, or blow air into his face, or even catch him as he was falling and push him back up.

Brother Odo's story emerged in fragments, in between sleeping and waking, through fever and eating, during the course of the next two days as we slowly made our way westward.

When he saw me disappear into the ground, dragged down by white hands, he had naturally assumed that I had been taken by demons and pulled down into the pit. Although he didn't remember what he had said then, I did, for they were the last words I heard before losing consciousness myself.

"The devil, the devil, the devil has risen from Hell, run, run, run!"

Brother Odo had taken his own advice and run, straight into the pursuing Danes. But such was his fear of Hell that not even the sight of the Danes had caused him to stop shouting his warning. They took him, but he kept screaming his warning and, although he did not say this I could add it, such was the power and simplicity of his fear that even the Danes began to fear Hell's rising, and look askance upon each other, sensing some evil spirits abroad.

But though the Danes feared devils much, they feared the sons of Ragnarr more: they had been sent in pursuit of me and the Book, and they began to put Brother Odo to the question as to where I was, and the Book.

Of course, he told them. I had been dragged down to Hell and the Book with me. Although the Danes tried to take Brother Odo to show them where this had happened, such was his fear at the approach to the place that even the Danes only approached to a distance. Seeing it bare and there being nowhere for a man to hide, they had heeded their own fear and retreated to a distance to take counsel.

All through this time, Brother Odo told me, he had been praying that God would take him and release me from the bonds of Hell. With any other monk, I would have taken this as mere pious hypocrisy but with Brother Odo I knew it to be no more than the simple truth.

The Danes' council was disturbed by their sighting, in the woods and copses around Rohesia's Cross, some of the inhabitants of the village. In response, some of the Danes set off in pursuit. The remnant, reduced, grew all the more nervous at Brother Odo's continued warnings that the devil had risen and would drag them down to Hell. So when one of the Danes suggested making a sacrifice to the chief of their gods, Odin, followed by a swift departure to a less wraith-haunted place, they had swiftly agreed.

Which was how Brother Odo found himself tied to an ash tree, crucified, after the manner of our God, and hanging, after the manner of theirs, for apparently the chief of their gods hung himself upon a great tree for nine days to gain great gifts of knowledge and power.

Left hanging from the tree, Brother Odo told me, in his fever ravings, how he offered up his sufferings for my salvation, welcoming the cold and the cramps and the struggle for each and every breath as sacrifice for me. In his long agony, he was comforted by the arrival of his donkey, Buttercup. The sensible beast must have avoided the Danes by hiding in one of the nearby woods, but once they had gone it had returned in search of its master. Finding Brother Odo, Buttercup had nuzzled him awake. Unable to free its master, the beast had remained with him, shielding him from the wind's blast with its body and warming him with its breath. It had even disappeared off, only to return a short while later with Wolfbait — although my animal apparently proved somewhat less capable as a nurse, generally forgetting its duties and wandering off to crop what grass it could find. They had only abandoned their post when the stinking apparition that was Gotho had appeared, as if from nowhere, prompting a sudden flight.

For his part, Brother Odo had taken Gotho for another demon, and prepared himself to be dragged down into Hell, only for the foul creature to disappear off in the other direction, stumbling and falling and coughing, until a loud splash told that he had found the water he had been looking for. The subsequent splashes and slowly receding cries suggested to me that Gotho had taken his own unwitting journey, downstream to the sea. It probably would take the ocean to clean him properly.

Then, Brother Odo had seen me, and his joy was great. His sacrifice had been accepted and I had been released from Hell. For my part, my sacrifices were just beginning. Over the course of the next few days of painfully slow travel, I had to care for him, cook for him, feed him and even put him to bed. Our lodgings were abandoned farms and falling down sheds, but at least they served to keep the worst of the winter wind and rain from us. Buttercup would even lie down by his master to provide him with warmth through the night.

Whatever else I am, I am no nursemaid. But if I have a besetting sin (other than such obvious candidates as lust, avarice and cowardice), it is curiosity. I could not leave him until I had learned what had happened to him and how he had survived being taken by a party of vengeful, pursuing Danes. Luckily for my brother monk, it took such a time to extract the story of his survival that by the time I knew it all, Brother Odo was much recovered and well enough to resume his duties. So I set him to preparing my meagre lunch as I turned my thought to what we should do next.

We had travelled some twenty miles west of Rohesia's Cross by winding ways, avoiding the great roads for they would, of a certainty, be patrolled and watched by the Danes. But if I would make faster time west and reach the kingdom of the West Saxons before the Danes, then I needed to travel faster, and the only way to do so was by road. Or river.

River. Water was the Danes' great highway. They came over the grey sea in their dragon boats, swift and deadly vessels that rode unscathed through storms that our own boats would founder in, and then when they came to our river-scored land, they rowed upstream to some easily defensible position, made camp there, and raided and plundered before making a swift withdrawal the way they had come. To risk the river was to risk the Danes.

But if I were to cut west, maybe one or two days' journey from where we were camped, I should meet the River Lea. Its broad and calm waters flowed due south to meet the River Thames not far downstream from the old Roman city, now left to ruin and rats. Rowing the Thames upstream would take me along the border between the kingdom of the West Saxons, on the south side of the river, and the kingdom of the Mercians, on the north side. There were no easily navigable rivers flowing into the heart of the kingdom of the West Saxons but that would be no matter: there were many royal settlements near the Thames as it flowed inland — there was one at Readingum much favoured by the West Saxon kings. Even if I did not find King Æthelred there, I would gain news of his whereabouts from his steward. And of course the great advantage of going upstream along the River Thames was that the river was tidal a long way inland: up to a small, mean settlement at Stane. This meant that even if I could not find boatmen to row me, all I had to do was wait for the tide to turn and I could let the river carry me upstream. Still, I did not anticipate a problem in finding rowers. There was a new settlement upriver of the Roman town and there you could always find avaricious men, willing to take you where you would so long as you guarded your purse and your life.

So, the river it was. By it, I might arrive in the kingdom of the West Saxons in three days; by land it were likely to take me the best part of two weeks.

Decision made, I looked at Brother Odo, sleeping next to Buttercup. Should I leave him? By the sound of his snoring — and that of the donkey — I could walk out of the shed we were sleeping in banging a drum and singing and he would not wake. But I had laboured to make him well; it would be stupid to waste the service he might offer me.

I kicked him.

"Get up," I said. "Pack. We're leaving."

Chapter 12

The River Lea ran south, broad and firm, its banks thick with willows trailing their dark branches in the grey winter water. The river's shores were tangled with marsh and carr, through which we picked our way, cursing whenever the surface layer of ice broke to send us into the freezing mud beneath. I needed to find a settlement where I might hire, or borrow, a boat, so we headed downstream, eventually finding a poor path that at least spared us the regular stumbles into freezing mud.

Brother Odo recited the Office as we went; for my part, I mumbled a litany of curses and complaints. The path was so poor that I could not even ride Wolfbait, for fear that he would stumble into a pothole and break a leg. Then the grey clouds decided to unload their contents as sleet. There is, in my experience, nothing so calculated to make a journey miserable than to undertake it in sleet; it freezes and soaks as nothing else does. When my cloak was sodden, I demanded Brother Odo's, but it was no better, so I flung it back to him, telling him to keep it dry for me next time, then stumbled on, foul tempered, wet and cold.

Which is often when my lady fortune most favours me. She must have a particular love for men in ill mood, for she has oft turned my fortune around when I have been in such humour: mayhap she prefers my normal sanguine temperament and would fain see its return.

A faint cry, and groaning. At first, I thought it was Brother Odo, and trudged onwards. But then it came again, and at the same time I realised that Brother Odo never complained or groaned against his fate. I looked up, receiving a slap of sleet full in my face, and turned my head, listening.

There, it came again. To our right, and ahead, from nearer the river. I held up my hand for Brother Odo to stop. Unfortunately, because he was walking with his head down and his hood up, he did not see my stopping hand and walked into me.

"Sorry, Brother Master, I did not see you," he said.

I shut him up with a gesture. "Do you hear?"

"Hear what?"

"Hear that."

The sound came again, more distinct and closer now. Groans. Human groans, of pain and distress.

There might be something to gain there.

I tied Wolfbait's reins to the nearest stand of willow, gestured for Brother Odo to do the same with Buttercup, then began to make my way cautiously through the screen of willow that separated us from the river. Off the path, my feet squelched deep into mud, while the willow wands, once pushed aside, slapped back into the face and body of the following Brother Odo with the sound of whip on leather. If he could not be quiet in his approach, I was at least grateful for his discipline, for he barely gasped, and then quietly, under the willow's lash. But it did mean that there was no chance of us making an approach in stealth.

However, as we got closer and the groans and cries grew louder, I became more confident that we did not need to approach in stealth: no one making those sorts of sounds would be in any condition to do us harm.

So it proved. For I broke through the final layer of willow and bulrush to find a boat, a good-sized vessel suitable for rivers and estuaries, tangled in the outgrowth of alder and willow by one of its oars. The sound was coming from within the boat.

I approached with what caution I could manage, having first looked carefully to see that there was no one waiting in hiding near the boat.

Satisfied that this was no trap, I made my way to the boat, until I was as close as the bank would take me. It was close enough.

The Danes, maybe one of the parties searching for me, must have found this boat. They had left only blood, and body parts, and one man alive, albeit barely, to tell the story of what remained of his companions. I am not a man given to compassion, but even I would not have wished the fate given to one of the men on the boat, whom the Danes had turned into a mockery of the dragon prows they carve on their own boats, setting him bottom high at its front. The one man living, hearing my approach, turned his remaining eye towards me and held up his hand in supplication.

"For a mercy," he begged.

The Danes would have left nothing of value. I turned away.

Brother Odo, following, his face pale and pinched at what he saw, looked to me. "Will we not give these men proper burial, Brother Master?"

"Do you want to gather up the pieces?" I asked him, making to push past. Which was a stupid question, because of course Brother Odo would gather up the pieces, and put them together again with all the loving devotion he offered to all, living or dead. But before he had time to answer, I heard something from the boat that made me think there was some worth in entering the charnel boat after all.

"Th-the bishop."

The words were weak but quite distinct. I turned back. The survivor was waving at us, from his position near the stern of the boat.

"What bishop?" I called, from where I stood. But the answer was too quiet for me to hear, although the man seemed to gesture within the boat.

I looked at Brother Odo. "You first."

So with Brother Odo carefully and reverently moving the bodies and assembling the body parts, I followed, attempting to breathe only through my mouth. For a mercy it was winter. In summer, I could never have approached.

The survivor lay in the stern. One of his eyes was missing, but the other looked up at us with something approaching hope. Quite what hope he might have in such a situation, when the life's blood was slowly draining from him, was unclear to me, yet there it was.

"What bishop?" I repeated.

The man coughed. From the colour of it, he had little time to live. So I squatted down next to him so that he could see me more clearly and I could hear him better.

"What bishop?"

The man grabbed my arm, pulling his ruined face towards me. I would rather it had not been so close, but I could see the desperation to tell his story before death took him. Besides, there might be news of value to me in what he had to say.

"I-I am a monk," he began, "c-clerk to the new bishop, come from Rome."

Now *this* was interesting. A bishop from Rome would travel with great treasure and gifts for his new diocese.

"The Danes took us, as we rowed up the river, and despoiled us, killing all save me, then setting the boat to drift."

I looked around. "Nice boat."

"They took the gold," said the man, gasping over each breath. "They took the treasure. They despoiled the books, and threw what they did not want in the river."

"Is there anything of value left?" This was all getting to seem the sort of task I'd set for Brother Odo: pointless and unpleasant.

"Th-the bishop's ring," the man said. "They left that."

It was my turn to grab him. A bishop's ring carried his authority and power; the wearer of such a ring might command abbots and priests and clerks, nuns — even kings.

"They-they mocked him before they killed him," said the clerk. "Asking him where his God was now. They cut his ring finger from him and, in greater mockery, pushed it into his nether end before setting him, there." The clerk raised a trembling hand and pointed towards the front of the ship.

I turned and saw. "Of course." The plump man, bottom pointing skywards, impaled upon the bowsprit, must have been the bishop. If what the clerk said was true, his ring, the sign and symbol of his authority, might still be on — well, *in* — his person.

"Brother Odo," I said. "I have a job for you."

Chapter 13

"Brother Master." I barely heard Brother Odo, as I was busy with the steering oar and plans of what we should do next. Besides, it was my general policy to ignore what Brother Odo said, as I have little patience with pious platitudes and happy thoughts. The monk was sitting amidships with the two animals, Wolfbait and Buttercup, keeping them calm on the uncertain surface of a boat sailing upriver on the rising tide. I've seen many a vessel capsize when its animal cargo panicked at some slight shifting of the deck, but such was the regard with which the beasts held Brother Odo that they barely shifted the whole time they were aboard our boat, and then only to nuzzle the monk. Around us, the Thames flowed brown and strong. We had taken the bishop's boat, after Brother Odo had cleaned it and buried the dead with as much haste as I could cajole from him — which was quite a lot, when I boarded the boat and threatened to leave at once if he didn't hurry up. The journey downstream had been swift and, meeting the Thames, fortune favoured us with the tide, so that we rode its rising upriver. Brother Odo, manning the oars, sculled but his pulling mainly served to hold us in the right direction as we let the tide carry us inland. We had another three hours to make what progress we could before the tide turned and we would have to tie up and wait for its next turning. The tide ran upstream to Stane and I was planning to make use of it as far as possible. After that? Well, Brother Odo was proving to be a skilled oarsman. It wasn't that far upstream from Stane to Readingum.

"Brother Master." Brother Odo repeated his importuning. There was in his words the special note of pleading that indicated he really had something to say to me, although that usually consisted of some ridiculously stretched application of Scripture to the situation in which we found ourselves. But occasionally it was something important, so I looked from my careful watch of the river's banks to the monk. His expression was unusual: strained and hesitant. He looked to be struggling with his bowels.

"I can't stop," I said. "Do it over the side. There's no one watching, and even if there was, all they'd see would be the scrawny bottom of a monk; they see that all the time."

"No, no, Brother Master, that is not what I would speak of."

"What then?" I sighed, turning my attention back to the river watch. He was going to speak some scruple. How tiresome.

"You know I do not carp at the duties you place upon me, Brother Master, for I consider your commands as binding upon me as those of the Abbot, or Holy Mother Church." Brother Odo paused.

I sighed again. Oh, great, he wanted reassurance that he was as self-effacing and humble as he thought himself to be. "Yes, I know," I said.

"So I say this not lightly, Brother Master, but only after great thought and searching of heart. But you should not have asked me to take the bishop's finger from his arse. It was not right. It was not dignified — not for me, of course, that is not my concern, but for the late bishop."

"But who else was going to do it? Not me."

"We — we could have left it where it was?"

"What, this?" I held up my right hand. On it was the bishop's ring — I'd had Brother Odo clean it thoroughly after extracting it. "The sign and symbol of a bishop's authority, the authority vested in him through the mandate of Our Lord, passed on to the Apostles, and you wanted to leave it up his arse?"

"No, no," said Brother Odo. "But it was not right that I should have to take it from there."

"Tell that to the Danes. They're the ones who put it there. Or tell it to God: He's the one who gave the pagans leave to ravage this country."

Brother Odo looked shocked. "Brother Master!" he said.

I confess, my greatest temptation was to laugh. After all that I had asked of him, this was what had first caused Brother Odo to whisper pause. But the delicacies of the human soul are strange and curious: a man might push through mounds of entrails only to stop at the sight of a whining dog.

"Haven't you thought on that?" I asked. "We, who were pagans, have been Christian these past two centuries, sending men of our kin to convert our pagan cousins in Frisia and Germania, only for God to send new pagans to lay our country waste. Does it seem fair to you?"

"It must be because of some great sin that we have committed that He has sent the Danes, as a scourge and goad to us."

"Well, I don't know of any sin that I have committed that deserves monasteries laid waste, women violated, children taken as slaves and men left to die with their own finger shoved up their arse, but maybe you've committed some sins worthy of such punishment." I looked to Brother Odo. "You had better confess."

Brother Odo looked stricken. "Do you think it is for *my* sin that such punishment is meted upon us?" he asked.

I was sore tempted to tell him yes, but the answer, as I saw it, lay heavy upon my heart and I spoke it.

"No, no."

"Then for why does God send such punishment down upon us?"

"I know that no more than I know how the seas rise and fall twice each day."

"But there must be some reason why God should allow this to befall us. For the Fathers say that while He does not will evil, He permits it."

I looked around. The country north of the river lay empty and bare, the houses and people that had once made of it a fertile and pleasant land gone. The Danes had left only a wasteland.

"He's permitting a lot of it at the moment."

Chapter 14

I was a bishop. Sailing upstream, letting the tide and Brother Odo do the work, I looked at the ring sitting proud on my finger. All right, I was a bishop without a diocese — the clerk had lived long enough to tell me where to find the bishop's ring but not long enough to say where that ring was going — but there was always a demand for a good bishop. After all, what with the raids and the slave taking of the Danes, half the bishoprics in the realms of the Angles and the Saxons lay vacant, and a fair few in the land of the Britons too. Not many bishops had survived the fall of their lord's kingdom, although rumour had it that wily old Wulfnoth, bishop of York and the second most senior priest in Britain after Canterbury, was rubbing along perfectly well with his new Norse king. But in most dioceses, the bishop's chair sat vacant. My bottom would fit very nicely into one of those chairs. What's more, as bishop I would have legitimate reason to keep the Book — and if the abbey at Medeshamstede was ever restored, as bishop I would have the power to deny any petition they might make to recover it.

So, all I had to do was get to Æthelred, king of the West Saxons, present my ring, trot out some story of a Danish attack in which I had lost the other members of my household and my documentation, but which, by the Grace of God, I had survived, and put myself forward as a bishop at his bidding. Kings were always glad to install like-minded bishops in important bishoprics. It helped to ensure the smooth running of the kingdom. And I intended to make sure that everything ran very smoothly indeed.

"Brother Odo, can't you row any faster?" It was cold, with a wind blowing from the east that knifed through my cloak however tightly I pulled it round my shoulders.

"Y-yes, Brother Master," Brother Odo panted, pulling his stroke further into the dark water. Despite the cold, there was a sheen of sweat on Brother Odo's brow.

"Think yourself blessed that you do not have to suffer the cold of this wind, as I have to," I said to Brother Odo. I made a slight adjustment to the rudder, exposing as little of my hand to the wind as possible.

"Th-thank you, B-Brother Master," said Brother Odo.

We were making good progress upriver. We had passed the water meads of Fulanham and the eyots at Twicanhom, and we were approaching the rich, fat meadows of Stane. The north bank of the river remained sullen and unpopulated, a wasted and overgrown land, where fields lay unploughed and fallow, populated only by the occasional wary goat or thoughtful cow. But the south bank was still an inhabited although watchful land. As we rowed, I saw watchmen, hidden in thickets and copses, take note of our progress, sending runners off after we had passed to tell of our coming. But a single boat with two men, a horse and a donkey does not an invasion of the Danes make: we were not hailed or stopped. For my part, I intended that we should go as far upriver as Readingum and there make land, asking in the royal cantonment there for the location of King Æthelred and his brother, Alfred.

That was the plan. It did not work out that way.

We had moored, in the cover of a dense stand of willow and alder, to wait out the turning of the tide and the roughly eight hours until the river, released, would flow downstream. I had given Brother Odo leave to sleep and taken watch myself — a mistake, as it turned out. Whenever I act with kindness it never works for the better, although my main reason for giving him a rest was that I had calculated that he could not row much further without a break. I think God or lady fortune must wish me to be what I am, for any slight move against my nature is always met with disaster.

So there I was, on watch, but it was reasonably sheltered among the trailing willow branches and steering a boat is hard work too. I drifted into sleep.

Only to be woken from a particularly pleasant dream of a visit, in my bishop's mitre, to a convent of nuns eager to please, by a loud call.

"Oi, you! We paid for those horses. Get rowing."

I shook awake, and even in my waking I knew there was something odd about that call. Then I looked, and saw it came from a man standing in the prow of a dragon boat, holding on to the evil worm that leered from the front of the vessel, and pointing up stream, and I realised that what I had heard strange was the call in Norse.

The Danes were come.

Looking, fearfully, beyond, I saw the river thick with their boats, and others, small vessels, laden with supplies or carrying horses, crewed by men wearing the iron collars of slaves.

The Danes were come to take the last of the kingdoms of England, and we had fallen among them.

"Get moving," the Dane yelled again, before he signalled and his men gave one stroke on the starboard side of the boat to pull it back into the stream. But, there, he waited, watching.

Thus began the evillest day of my memory — well, since the last evil day, which was when I was dragged into Gotho's pit. Or the day when King Edmund had tied me to a pillar as sacrifice to the Danes. Or the night when I was happily tupping my wife, only to be pulled off her by my twin brother claiming to be me — and my wife corroborated him. Which was how I found myself carried into Medeshamstede as an adulterer and oath breaker. For one whom fortune favours, I seem to suffer evil days all too regularly.

We had to pull, upstream, against the full force of the river's renewed flow as it sought to send all the water that had been pushed upstream by the tide back down to the sea. The Danes, however, swept past us in their boats, yelling for us to make more speed. For a while I entertained the hope that we might simply slip backwards through their fleet but as we neared the rear, I saw that they had stationed a few small, swift rowing boats there to act as guards and goads to the collection of slow, reluctantly rowed boats that made up the tail end of their fleet.

Looking round, seeing the exhausted faces and bent backs in the boats around us, all the men wearing the iron collars of slaves, I realised that to be numbered among them was to consign myself to their fate. We had to make our way forward, and join the main body of the fleet. For I had also noticed that among the Danes were others: freebooters, Frisians, Franks and men from further afield. But these were not only men who had come over sea for gold and plunder; unless I was much mistaken, rowing in among the Danish fleet were many Angles and Saxons too. What's more, they were rowing freely, without the iron collar. Some among my fellow countrymen had decided to take Norse lords for themselves and fight for the sea reivers. Thus, they sought to become land masters. Seeing as how the Danes had already taken two of the ancient kingdoms and neutered a third, their decision appeared wise.

If I was to number myself among the free followers of the Danes, and thus have some chance to escape them, I had to get away from where the slaves and prisoners laboured at the back of the fleet.

"Row, Brother Odo, row," I said.

"I — am — rowing," gasped Brother Odo.

"Row faster," I said.

"I — will — try," said Brother Odo. Sitting at the helm, I saw him bend into his stroke, the sweat, despite the cold, running down his face, but we barely made any more progress than before. We were slipping further back. Soon, we would be in the rearmost rank, prey to the attention of the guard boats there.

"Faster," I said. "I will call the rhythm."

So I began calling the strokes, increasing the pace to near double that of the boats around us, but still we were only holding our own place in the fleet.

"Are you malingering, Brother Odo?"

He looked up at me, his eyes dark amid the sweat sheen, and shook his head. And to my horror I realised that if I wanted to move the boat further up the fleet, then I would have to take an oar myself.

That was when the real evil of the day began.

I have ridden through day and night; I have walked for days and weeks; I have fought, reluctantly, in battles and fallen exhausted to the ground afterwards. But nothing else compares to rowing upstream for six hours in the middle of a Danish invasion fleet. By the end, I could barely move and, when the fleet made land at Readingum, I had scarce the strength to notice that the Danes had stopped where I had planned to stop myself. Nor did I realise at first that what I had thought an invasion fleet was merely reinforcements: the Danes were already camped at Readingum. Brother Odo had to peel my fingers from the oars, lift me from the rowing bench and carry me ashore, where he left me to slowly uncurl my seized-up back beside Buttercup and Wolfbait, while he set to with the digging the Danes required of all the men landing, including their own.

They had drawn their boats up on the strand where the River Kennet met the Thames and, to protect the camp, they dug an earthwork between the two rivers, creating a triangular enclosure about three acres in extent. As I lay beside the beasts, I saw the signal fires flaring deep into the kingdom of the West Saxons. Their king would soon know, if he did not already, that the Danes were come to take his kingdom.

When, at last, I could move faster than a tree, I took myself to learn what I might. Speaking their language, I can move among the Danes not as one of their own but as a man oath sworn to them, for normally only such speak their tongue. By the fortifications and preparations I saw around me, it was clear that this was no ordinary raid: they had come to conquer. Already foraging parties were spreading through the near country, looking for provisions.

That was when I learned something new about myself. I had not thought of myself as particularly attached to my people. Yes, I was of their blood, but the passions that moved them were not mine: I cared not a jot for battles, save to survive them, and God's work I would leave to monks and priests (admittedly, I was now a monk and, hopefully, a bishop, but God could look after his own business and I would look to mine). So I thought to care little that the Danes were taking the land, save to profit and escape from it. But when a ruckus went up near the gate to the camp, and I went to see what had happened, I heard the tale in the shouts and oaths of the men bringing in a few battered, blood-stained bodies. One of the raiding parties had been attacked and its men killed. The Danes, bringing their dead in, swore oaths of vengeance but

I, seeing the hacked bodies, felt a curious thrill that I could not at first identify until I realised that it was gladness at finally seeing the Danes bested and their men being dragged back to camp on willow hurdles.

It was probably this unfamiliar emotion that caused me to drop my attention to the men around, otherwise I would have slipped quietly away. But, as it was, a voice hailed me.

"Slaver! You are here."

I turned at the call, my bowels griping as I recognised the voice hailing me, then turning to water as my eyes confirmed my ears.

Earl Thorgrim, standing tall among the giants of his house guard, was waving me over.

I confess, my legs would have taken me in terror flight from the earl if they had not been rendered so weak that I could barely stand. But it was as well that they failed me, for I knew well that flight, in such a place, would be my death. Attempting to settle my stomach, I waved in answer and began to walk towards Thorgrim.

But the earl came to me and, reaching me, buffeted me round the shoulders in a greeting that was meant to be friendly but probably would have entitled me to a payment of ten silver pennies under the laws of King Ine.

"Come to fill your bucket with what we take in Wessex, Slaver?" Thorgrim said. "I'm still counting what you earned me from the monks of Medeshamstede; I'd never have got so much selling them myself."

"It always pays to get a specialist to do the job: a slaver for selling and buying slaves…"

"…and a Dane for taking them," finished Thorgrim. "It's good to see you again, Conrad. There'll be plenty of slaves for the selling by the time we're through with the West Saxons. But how did you end up at the court of the king of the East Angles? I hear his ending was long."

"So I hear also," I said, carefully. "But I was there for the same reason that I am here: to gather slaves for market. Only, I found that I had arrived either too early — for you had not yet come in strength to take the kingdom — or too late, for looking around I saw few that would fetch a good price in market. You must have cleared the kingdom of its best stock when you were there before."

Earl Thorgrim laughed. "We did indeed. The young men either joined us, or we took them for selling. As for the young women," he laughed again, "we just took them."

"What of the king, Ivarr? Where is he? I have not seen him, though I thought for sure he would be leading the Great Army. For the kingdom of the West Saxons is the last to stand against you."

"Him? Ivarr the Bastard! He's gone. Upped and left us. Had word that his holdings in Dubhlinn and the north were under threat and sailed off, just like that. Pah." Thorgrim spat on the ground. "We don't need him." Thorgrim leaned down to me, putting his hand on my shoulder, and whispered, "Besides, now he's gone, I can tell you how he got his name. He'd kill any man he catches telling the story, but now he's leagues away, I can say it. He'd taken this woman, see, one of your nuns. Beautiful and noble and a virgin. So after Ivarr had drunk, he thought to take her, but this nun, when he found her, was kneeling, praying, and she was praying that he might not take her. So Ivarr strips her but she's still praying and praying and crying out to your god and then, when he drops his breeches, he can't get it up. No matter how he tries, and she's as beautiful a woman as you've ever seen, he can't get a bone there. And that's how he got his name. You can see why he doesn't much like it."

"Yes." I nodded. "What happened to the nun afterwards?"

"Oh, he cut her, so she wasn't beautiful any more, then gave her to be sold. Don't know where she went. Probably to Dubhlinn, to the slave markets there. It's another reason why he hates your god. Me, I don't care much one way or another, but I don't see what there is to worship in a god that stops a man getting it up."

"The priests say there is more to it than that but, for my part, I sometimes think you're right: our religion is mostly about stopping a man getting it up."

"That's what I thought. And what's the good of that? By the way, I bought one of your slaves myself and he's proved extremely useful, what with his reading and writing. I'll call him over." Thorgrim turned and whistled and a small man came bustling over, a man who became increasingly, horrifyingly clearer as he approached.

"Abbot Flory," I said. "How good to see you again."

The abbot stared at me. The colour drained from his face and his mouth began to work, but only sounds, that might have been sobs or gasps of rage, came from his lips. Then he began to shake, as if he had the dropsy.

Thorgrim, watching our meeting, looked to me. "There, I knew he would be pleased to meet you again. I will leave you to speak for a minute but come when I call, Flory, for I will have need of you soon."

Abbot Flory remained speechless, stuttering with rage, so I thought to speak in Thorgrim's absence.

"Abbot Flory, I know you will be tempted to denounce me to the earl but before you do so, ask yourself this one question: do you want the Danes to have the Book?"

Abbot Flory, already as pale as chalk, became even paler. He grabbed my arm. "You-you have the Book?"

"Yes," I said. "It is safe. But if you speak one word against me, I shall hand it over to the Danes, and they will despoil it. So, you have a choice, Abbot Flory: allow the temptation to revenge to overpower you and thus consign yourself to Hell, or preserve your life's work and save your soul. What do you say?"

The abbot stared at me, the emotions churning through his face, his fingers biting into my arm as if they were teeth. But I gave no hint of the pain they caused me, nor did I let any of the fear that gripped me show on my face.

The abbot let go of my arm. His head dropped.

"I will not speak against you. Save only the Book."

"Good," I said. "You have chosen wisely, for the sake of your soul and our common faith. But it is not the Book only that I saved: I have Brother Odo with me too."

"Odo?" Abbot Flory looked round. "Where?"

"He is tending to the animals but I will send him over to speak with you when there is time." I pointed. Earl Thorgrim was looking to us, and waving. "You are required, Abbot Flory. Trot along."

The abbot looked round with all the fright of an ignorant novice in Medeshamstede then, seeing the earl's gesture, shouted, "Coming," and scurried off.

I returned to Brother Odo.

"You know my plan? It's working."

Chapter 15

We could not stay with the Danes. Telling Flory that I had the Book had bought me a little time, but soon the worms of plotting would start to gnaw at the abbot, and he would turn to thinking how he might win back the Book and bring about my downfall at the same time. No, we had to get away.

But for the first few days, no opportunity presented itself. The Danes were busy making their camp secure, digging ditches and throwing up earth ramparts topped with fences and stakes. Everyone in the camp was called on to help in the work.

For my part, I can safely say that I am not made for a life of labour. Each night I fell exhausted asleep, more dead than alive, thinking as sleep took me whether it were better to simply unmask myself to the Danes and bring an end to this rather than endure another day. But by the fourth day, the building was finished, the Danes were secure in their camp, with their boats dragged up upon the shore ready for a quick escape should the camp's defences fail, and they turned their thoughts once more to provisioning.

Raiding parties set out, riding swiftly over the winter land, seeking farms and villages and housesteads. But the demands of a thousand men, not to mention their horses, are great, and soon the raiding parties had to venture further and further from the camp.

That was when Thorgrim called me to his tent.

"You have some knowledge of this land, Conrad, and its people. Halfdan has given me the task of provisioning the army, but the men he's given to me to do so are fools who would miss a pig unless they fell over it. I want you to go with the next provision expedition; tell them where your farmers store their harvest and hide their animals; take them to the settlements, so that they don't have to ride around for hours looking."

It is a good idea never to appear delighted when the opportunity you have craved drops into your lap.

I shook my head. "I know only a little of this land, lord. Surely another would better serve?"

"No," said Thorgrim. "I need someone I know will return."

"And you know I will return?"

"Of course. You would not turn aside from the gold our slave taking will bring you."

I affected to look affronted. "You think I care only for gold, my lord?"

Thorgrim looked closely at me. "Not only. But mostly."

I made to bow. "They say the Danes see deep into a man's soul. You have judged mine well: mostly gold."

Thorgrim nodded. "We Danes see true, for life depends upon the man standing beside you in the shield wall."

I made no answer, and waited.

Thorgrim looked searchingly upon me once more, as if searching for my soul. I looked at the space above his eyes and waited.

"Flory says strange things about you. That you were a monk in his monastery, and betrayed your brethren, selling them into slavery. That you stole from them something of great value, a Book. What do you say to that, Slaver?"

I looked back at Earl Thorgrim.

"All true."

Thorgrim blinked. His hand moved to his sword hilt.

I held up my hand. "But there is no lie better than a truth distorted. Yes, I was a monk at his monastery — but an unwilling one, put there by my enemies. You saw for yourself, at the market, where my abilities lie, and I will put them to your service again, should you give me chance. As to the theft of the Book, of course I took it. As would you. But I'm afraid I no longer have it, for Ivarr took the Book from me, when he put an end to the kingdom of the East Angles."

Thorgrim nodded. "That bastard would take everything and call it his own: his thirst for gold is greater than a dragon's. For my part, I saw your work at the market: you are no monk. I will punish Flory for his false telling."

"When he was abbot, he gave me many strokes across the back. Such a punishment would not hurt the parts of him most valuable to you: his hands."

I rode out of the camp with the raiding party to the sound of willow wands thwacking bare flesh, and the barely suppressed whimpers of Abbot Flory. It was as sweet a music as I have heard.

Brother Odo, however, found the music less to his liking. At every thwack, he would start, as if the willow was cutting into his own back, and tears streamed down his face.

After the third stroke, he pulled Buttercup's head round with more violence than I had ever seen from him and made to urge the beast back to camp.

I grabbed the bridle just in time.

"Where are you going?" I hissed.

"I-I will offer myself in place of the Abbot. Let them punish me, who is unworthy, rather than he, who is holy."

"Don't be stupid," I said. "They'll just whip you as well."

"For why do the Danes punish the Abbot so?" he asked me, the tears streaming down his face.

"No doubt for his very holiness." When Brother Odo made a move to still return to camp, I pulled Buttercup closer. "Being so holy, Abbot Flory will exult in this unjust punishment and offer it for God's glory. Would you take such sweet suffering from him?"

That, I could see, broke Brother Odo's anguished empathy. If he had been subjected to such a lashing, Brother Odo would, I had no doubt, have seen it as a chance to lay his suffering at the foot of the Cross. While I suspected that Abbot Flory was laying his pains at my feet, Brother Odo would not know that, and I did not intend that we should return to camp for him to find out the truth.

Brother Odo nodded. "You are right as ever, Brother Master. In my secret pride I would have taken the glory of his suffering from Abbot Flory and claimed it for myself." He looked at me, his eyes still shining wet with his tears, but also a new emotion, one that I could not immediately identify.

"How fortunate I am to have you as my spiritual master, Brother Master, for you lay bare to me the duplicity of my soul and keep me from all the secret vices the enemy would snare me with." And he bent down to my hand and kissed it.

Which was when I realised what that emotion was: gratitude. The reason for my failure to recognise it became clear. I had not seen gratitude directed towards me very often.

Chapter 16

We rode from the camp of the Danes, heading south by an old foot-path that marked one of the ancient ways of the people of this land. The hamlets and farms nearest the camp had already been laid waste, of course, so we rode past them without stopping, although Brother Odo whispered blessings as we passed for the people displaced, and signed the cross over the occasional body lying broken by a burnt-out building. The Danes did not normally kill the people they raided but those who resisted were cut down at once as warning to others to hand over their winter stores. Death might then come later in the season, through the slow wasting of flesh. But death, the Danes wanted all the farmers and villagers to know, would come on the instant if they tried to withhold their winter stores. Most learned the lesson well, it seemed, for I saw few bodies as we went, and fewer people, as the lesson the farmers and villagers learned best of all was to flee when word came that the Danes were near.

Before we had gone too far, I determined to test the reins that held me. The Dane leading our raiding party was a sour-faced man whose shoulders were wider than his horse's girth. He was named Smiler Olaf, I was told, because he only smiled when he killed. Well, I would see if

I could make him smile for a different reason and ease the guard upon me, with a view to escaping as we rode deeper into the kingdom of the West Saxons.

I urged Wolfbait up the column until we were just behind Smiler Olaf, in which position I groaned. When Smiler Olaf did not look round, I groaned again… and louder. When he still did not look round I groaned once more, then eased the groan into a gasp of suppressed pain — the sort of sound a brave man might make when enduring unendurable agony.

"All right," said Smiler Olaf, still not looking round, but at least speaking to me, "what is it?"

I urged Wolfbait closer to the huge Norse so that I could better whisper my reply.

"Piles."

"How big is yours?" asked Smiler Olaf.

"Oh, about the size of a finger," I said. I was making this up, of course. How big did piles get? I was about to find out the answer.

"I had one bigger than my thumb," said Smiler Olaf, and now he looked round to me, which was probably even more alarming than when he had been ignoring me, for his face was twisted into a strange, curled shape that I could not interpret.

"Really?" I said.

The Dane's face twisted even more and I suddenly realised what Smiler Olaf was trying, and failing, to do. He was trying to smile.

"Yes, really. Hurt worse than getting stabbed. Do you want to know how I got rid of mine?"

"Oh, yes. Please."

"Turnips," he said.

"Turnips?"

"Yes, turnips. No more red meat and lots of turnips. Eat them, then find a good-sized one and use it to push it back in."

"*Back in?*" I squeaked.

"Yes." Smiler Olaf's face twisted up even more in his hideous attempt at smiling. "Do you want me to help?"

"Er, maybe later."

"Oh." His face curled up even more in his ghastly smile. "You sure?"

"Once I've been off the red meat for a week, you'll be the first person I'll ask to help me with my turnip."

"Good, good. Not easy to do the turnip on your own."

"I'm sure it isn't." I paused. "Would it be all right for me to stop and ease myself?"

Smiler Olaf nodded. He appeared to be trying to look sympathetic although any child seeing the expression would like as not have suffered nightmares for the week afterward. "I always found riding made me want to go."

"Yes, me too. Would it be all right if I had a little privacy? You know how it is?"

"Of course. Last thing anyone with piles wants is an audience when they're trying to go." Smiler Olaf held up his hand, calling the riders to a halt. "We'll wait for you here."

"That's kind. I was afraid I might lose you otherwise."

"Tell me. Sometimes it would take me half the day to get it out."

I nodded my thanks, then dismounted Wolfbait and made my bow-legged approach towards a nearby brake of trees that marked the lip of the next ridge of land. Pushing in through the hawthorn and hazel that lined the edge of the copse so that I was concealed, I looked back. The Danes were waiting, sat on their horses, with Brother Odo at the rear on Buttercup. So no chance of an escape, but I had established that there was a previously unsuspected sympathy between people with piles. Each time I needed to go, I would pull the leash further until, finally, when we were far from camp and I had Wolfbait near, I would slip away.

Rolling my plan contentedly through my mind, I realised that, though my bowels were clear, my bladder was beginning to strain. I undid my trousers and, stepping on to the edge of a long ditch, began to relieve myself, looking absent mindedly at the land rolling into the distance beyond.

So it took a few moments for me to register that my piss, steaming through the winter air into the ditch, was making a strange sound as it splashed on to the ground. Rather than the rattle of piss on dry leaves, or the hiss of it falling on frostbound earth, it was making a ringing sound, as if it was falling on metal.

Slowly, with an unexpected dread at what I might see beginning to clutch at my heart, I looked down. Surely a man might ease his bladder in peace?

Apparently not. For looking down, I looked into the eyes of a man raising his head to look up at me. I had been pissing on his helmet. As he raised the visor and I saw his face, I knew that this was no ordinary helmet, for the face guard was richly worked into the likeness of the face of the man wearing it, a young man with ash eyes and a straggly beard and yellow beads of my piss trickling down his cheek. The men either side of him were starting to look up as well and, from the corner of my eyes, I saw that there was a line of men filing through the ditch, using it as cover to move without being seen through the winter landscape. Until I pissed on them.

I didn't wait. In my experience, men respond badly to being pissed upon, and even worse when they're armed and there's a lot of them. I turned round and began running back towards Smiler Olaf. As I picked my legs up, the thought occurred to me that this was the first time in my life I had ever run towards a group of Danes.

But the picking up of my legs proved a problem in my escape. In my haste, I had forgotten that I'd undone my trousers in order to do my fateful piss. Loosed, they had pooled round my ankles and, as I emerged, yelling, from the brake of trees, my trousers brought me down. As I fell, I saw that my cry had reached the Danes, for I saw men turning their horses towards me, but before I could gather my trousers and get up, a foot slammed me back into the ground. All around, men rushed past me, racing towards the Danes. Smiler Olaf, no longer smiling, yelled the retreat, and the Danes pulled their horses' heads back towards the camp, fleeing before the missiles and arrows of the pursuing West Saxons. I knew they were West Saxons from the curses I heard around me, as they called fury that they had been discovered. On foot, they had no chance of catching Smiler Olaf and his men.

The foot on my back was removed. Unfortunately, it was replaced by the hard point of a sword.

"You pissed on me, Dane. Now I'm going to kill you."

And I felt the sword beginning to press into my spine and I knew I was going to die if my words did not stop it.

"I'm a bishop, not a Dane."

The pointed pressure on my back released.

"Turn over."

I rolled on to my back. The man I had pissed on stood over me, his sword pointed now at the centre of my chest.

"Why would a bishop be part of a Danish raiding party and piss on me?"

The eyes that looked down upon me were cold but clear. I had seen eyes like that before. They opened on to a mind on which the red mist of battle did not descend, but rather the chill of winter sight. This was a man whose vision became clear when those around him descended into battle madness.

"Do you think I had any choice? As for the unfortunate accident, I didn't know you were there."

The man shook his head. "Still nothing that tells me the truth of what you claim."

I held up my hand, with the bishop's ring on it. His eyes narrowed when he saw it, but he shook his head again.

"A ring may be taken from the hand that wears it."

I felt the sword press harder into my chest.

"In principio erat Verbum et Verbum erat apud Deum et Deus erat Verbum." I said the Latin as firmly and clearly as I could, and I saw his eyes widen in recognition of the words. "Would a Dane know the holy tongue?" I asked.

The pressure lessened slightly, but the sword was still poised above my heart.

"For a shame, I know not the holy tongue myself. Those words sound holy to me, but tell them me in the vulgar tongue, that I might know you speak truly."

For the first and only time in my life, I silently thanked Abbot Flory for the Latin lessons he had made me endure during my time at Medeshamstede.

"In the beginning was the Word, and the Word was with God and the Word was God. The beginning of the Gospel of John."

As the words rolled from my tongue, I saw the man nod slowly.

"I know these words," he said. "You speak truly: no Dane would know them." Stepping back, he sheathed his sword. "Stand." A brief smile passed over his face. "But best to pull your trousers up first."

I struggled to my feet, pulling up my breeches as I stood. I was still tying them when I heard movement behind me.

"We got another one, but the rest escaped."

I glanced round to see that, despite escaping the Danes, I had not escaped my burden. Two of the West Saxons had Brother Odo, and they were dragging him towards the man on whom I had relieved myself.

"Brother Master!" Brother Odo managed a broad smile, despite the large bruise that was already swelling the left side of his face.

"You know him?"

I looked back to the man who was questioning me. For an instant I thought of finally ridding myself of the burden of Brother Odo but then I realised that, as a bishop, I would naturally have a retinue of monks and clerks. I could claim that most of mine had been killed by the Danes, but it was better to have at least one man to testify to my episcopal dignity.

Suppressing the sigh that came naturally before the acknowledgement, I said, "Yes, I know him."

"Brother Master, we are free!" said Brother Odo, and he dropped to his knees in prayer and praise.

I turned to my questioner. "We were cruelly used by the Danes, and we two alone survive of all the party that set out with me from Rome."

The man's face brightened. "You've been to Rome? I too, when I was but a boy." His gaze turned inwards as he relived precious memories. "Those were better days." He turned his grey eyes back upon me, his eyes thorn sharp once more. "Do they still light the candles in the Schola Saxonum that my father left money for?"

I coughed. It was the best I could think to do, for I saw the question was not asked idly. Although I had indeed been to Rome in my youth, and it had been as memorable a trip for me as it had been for my questioner, on my visit I had had more pressing calls upon my time than visiting the School of the Saxons on the Borgo di Santo Spirito; namely the avenue of Roman whores who, I was pleased to discover, did indeed live up to their reputation as the best but least generous whores in Christendom. I returned home spent in body and purse. I do not know why, but I find that the closer I am to holy places the greater my carnal appetites grow. It is probably as well that I have not made the pilgrimage to the Holy Land, for I fear my member might not survive the experience.

But I was saved making an answer by the arrival of more men, these running up to us with all the appearance of messengers.

"The king, your brother, calls for you."

I looked at the man to whom the message was addressed. So, I had pissed upon a prince. Fortune had blessed me once more, for few would survive pouring a yellow shower upon princely dignity — at least when unasked.

The prince looked to me and Brother Odo. "Come. You have been in the Danish camp. We would speak with you."

I held up my hand. "Of course I will come, and offer such knowledge as I can give. But I would know your name, prince…"

He looked at me, his eyes level and cool and sceptical. This, I realised, was a man who did not forget, one whom my usual charm would not convince.

"It is normal courtesy first to offer one's name to the lords of the kingdom you have entered. I will send you to the king, my brother, for introduction, and follow afterwards for I must first wash your own introduction to me away, lest I attend the king smelling of the sty. But as to me, I am named elf counsel. Alfred."

I made the courtesy to the young prince, silently giving thanks that he was not the king, for I suspected that I might find the gap between his reason and his credulity too small to slip through.

Alfred looked to the messengers. "Take these two to the king — I will follow very shortly."

The lead messenger looked to the prince. "The king would know why you do not come at his word."

Alfred pointed to me. "Let him tell the tale, after he has told his name and the king be satisfied of his truth."

Which was how I found myself telling the king of the West Saxons, to the king's increasing mirth, how I had pissed on his brother when planning my escape from the Danes.

My tale told, the king wiped the tears of laughter from his eyes and his cheeks.

"God's blood, would that I had been there to see that! Apple Alfred, the perfect prince, pissed upon in a ditch! I'd give you Canterbury for such a deed, if it were mine to give." Then he turned eyes that were suddenly sharp upon me. "It were almost worth telling the Danes we were here for such a thing. Almost."

"My lord, it was not of my willing that this happened. I have been long held by the Danes, and cruelly used by them. I was only seeking to escape. How could I know your brother was in the ditch below?"

"Indeed. How *could* you know?" The king stood up from his stool, his retainers, around him. He was, I saw with some discomfort, much taller than me, and his brother, Alfred. "I am Æthelred, king of the West Saxons, the last kingdom to stand before the Danes. In these years of woe, treachery and cowardice has ever been the friend of our foes, and our greatest bane."

I stood before the king with all the outraged innocence I could muster, which was a lot after my trials at the hands of the Danes, and put my hand to my heart, with the bishop's ring clearly on view. "If I stand false before you, a man who has been so ill used by the Danes, then let God strike me down where I stand."

King Æthelred looked at me with the same cold, grey regard as his younger brother.

"A ring may be taken and Latin learned. What other token do you bear to testify to your truth?"

As the king asked the fatal question, his brother arrived, his hair and face still wet from the washing. I saw the king's eyes lighten in amusement as they flicked to his brother, then return to me.

"Answer well, Conrad, for your life shall be forfeit if your answer does not satisfy me." He turned to Alfred, his eyes liquid with amusement though his mouth did not smile. "Or my brother, whom you have so gravely insulted."

I looked to the two young men with the same ice-grey eyes and knew that my life hung now upon a thinner thread than ever it had before. In such circumstances, I had learned that deeds served better than words — besides, I could feel my bowels griping and my throat drying with fear. Should I try to speak, my words would choke in my throat. So I beckoned. Brother Odo scurried forward. I whispered to him, then turned back to the king and prince and waited upon his return in silence.

I saw, from the swift glances they exchanged, that they had not expected such an answer from me. Still less did they expect what I drew from the bag that Brother Odo brought.

The Book.

The Gospel Book that had brought me through raid and capture and flight. It was, for me even more than them, a holy book.

They gasped at the sight of it, at the gold and garnets of its binding, at the colours, richer than life, of the pictures of the evangelists, and the richness of the design of the carpet page. The royal brothers looked up from the book to me, the man who had rescued it and brought it through so much peril, and their eyes shone with the wonder of it and, within, I felt fear's grip on my bowels loosen and my stomach relax.

"It is a wonder," said Alfred.

King Æthelred nodded. "You could give no greater token of truth than the book of truth itself. That you have saved it from the defiling hands of the pagans is a greater blessing than we could have looked for. One that makes worthwhile, the warning thereby given to our enemies of our presence. For we had looked to take the Danes by surprise, and attack their camp before they knew. Now, that will no longer be possible and I am minded that we should withdraw."

Before I could answer with a sober, episcopal assurance of the correctness of the king's judgement, Alfred said, "No!"

Both king and I turned to him.

"Why no?" asked Æthelred.

"Can you not see?" said Alfred, his face alight with the fervour of his belief. "This holy Book is a sign to us of God's favour. Surely He will deliver the Danes into our hands and render judgement against them, for He has brought the word of His truth to us through this," his words stumbled as his eyes flicked to me and I could see his tongue halt before pronouncing the usual appellation put before the title of bishop, that he was 'holy'. "This, er, fortunate bishop. We must act now, brother, and seize the fortune God has placed before us. What say you?"

And, with horror rising in my breast, I heard the king give his assent.

Chapter 17

"I — I was so sure that God was with us."

I looked at the pale, blood-streaked face of Prince Alfred and shook my head.

"It's been my experience that the moment people think God is really with them is the moment that he turns his face from them."

Alfred turned to me from where he was sitting, shocked and exhausted upon the tree stump that was the best seat his retainers could find for him.

"We were lucky. The Danes do not know this land as we do. We knew where to find the ford over the Kennet, and they did not. Else, there would have been no king left in the land, and it would have fallen to the Danes."

"Your brother, the king, he is well?"

"As well as a king defeated on the field might be. He has taken only slight injury, some cuts and bruises, but nothing to match the men we left behind for the ravens and the Danes." At these words, Alfred's eyes began to swim with tears. He made no move to brush them away, but let them fall to the ground.

"I should go to speak with him," I said.

Alfred nodded, his gaze falling away from me and back into bitter memory. "You were right," he said, quietly.

I stopped, and waited.

Without looking to me, he spoke on. "I saw that you would have advised against our attacking the camp of the Danes, but I was so sure that your coming to us with the Book was a sign and a token from God." He paused, staring into the frost-gripped earth, his breath misting around his face. "All my life I have searched for some sign from God of that which He would have me do. I thought, when I was old enough to have wit, that with four brothers elder to me I should enter the Church in His service. But then, I went with my father to Rome, and the Pope girt me with belt and sword, and in his holy basilica I saw, as if in vision, myself upon the throne. But how could this be, with four brothers?" Alfred shook his head. "It could be if they died. And though I loved them dear, die they did. First, Æthelstan, then Æthelbald, then Æthelberht, until only Æthelred is left between the throne and me. I would not take it: God knows this truly. In my heart, I would serve Him in other ways, but now I fear that He will bring about what he placed before my eyes those years ago in Rome. You understand my fear then, for my brother?"

"I understand," I said. "Although…what is clear to you may not be so apparent to others. To the head that wears the crown, it must seem that all men's hands are turned towards the taking it from him."

Alfred looked up at me, a startled expression on his face. "My brother thinks I would take the throne from him?"

"Maybe not take it, but from what he said he believes you were ever the favoured one of your parents."

Alfred shook his head. "Thus it might seem to him, but to me it seemed that I was always the one most expendable. So my father took me with him to Rome, for I was the youngest son, the one who would be least missed should I die upon the journey."

"But your mother?"

Alfred nodded. "Maybe there, Æthelred speaks with justice. But has it not ever been so, that a mother shall pet the child she had not hoped to bear?"

"Your brother, King Æthelred, is but few years older than you."

"And my mother had not thought to bear him. How much greater the surprise when I was conceived, out of time." Alfred stood up, stretching the pains and cuts from his limbs in the way that the very young can. If I had spent the day fighting with and then running from the Danes, I would have found it all but impossible to do anything else come the eve but to roll up, whimpering, in a corner. Thankfully, I had not taken part in the battle at Readingum, pleading the sanctity of my office and the weariness of my frame, but had watched, aghast, from afar, as the Danes had first engaged the attack and then, emerging from a hidden entrance to their barricades, had caught the West Saxons between two lines of warriors. It was little less than a miracle that Alfred and Æthelred had extracted so many of their men alive.

"I will come with you," said Alfred. "We must take thought on what to do."

It turned out that the first thing Æthelred thought to do, when we arrived at where he was camped with his retainers, was to grab me round the throat and start squeezing.

"Why didn't you tell us the Danes had another way out of their camp?" he snarled at me, his eyes popping with rage. "Are you a traitor, a spy?"

Normally I would have answered by some jest or pun, or suggested by supercilious silence that the question was beneath my episcopal dignity, but I could not speak due to the king's hands around my windpipe. Nor could I affect clerical outrage on account of dangling in the air from my neck. It was as well the king's brother was beside me, for he prevailed upon the king to put me down and, as a mist began to dim my eyes, I felt my feet again upon the ground and air once more in my lungs. I gasped, hands protectively around my neck, as King Æthelred glared down upon me, throwing me more questions.

I held up my hand in answer. "T-time." The word sounded like rough wood dragged across stone, and it felt even worse in my throat.

The king turned away in disgust to talk with his brother, while Brother Odo brought me a cup of ale, which I coughed up, and then a cup of sweet mead, which I didn't.

At last capable of speech, I turned to where the king stood among his retainers, warriors and counsellors, their voices all raised in a hubbub of recrimination and blame.

I raised my hand, a bishop asking for quiet that his word be heard, but the clamour did not die away, and few faces turned towards me.

I needed something to draw their attention. Or someone.

"Brother Odo…"

"Yes, Brother Master?" he turned to me, but his look of expectancy drained away as he saw my expression.

Really, he had no reason for such trepidation. All I was asking him to do was to draw the attention of the king. It was scarcely my fault that he chose to do this by marching in among the group of warriors surrounding the king, men tasked with protecting his person at the price of their own lives, and slapping Æthelred. Still, he survived, although somewhat bruised, and I got the attention of the king, his brother and all his retainers.

"I am a bishop, chosen by God, and you dared, you *dared* to choke my sacred person and accuse me of being a traitor!"

Good, they were all listening to me now.

"You ask why God gave the victory on this day to the Danes, and then you do this to one of his chosen! There, I have given you your answer. Now get down on your knees and beg for my — I mean God's — forgiveness."

I waited, staring at the blood-smeared, battle-battered group of men in front of me and slowly, one by one, they started going down on their knees. Brother Odo was already down, laid out flat by one of the king's retainers. Finally, only King Æthelred and his brother, Alfred, were left standing. Then Alfred, too, went down upon one knee.

"Why did you not give warning that there was another exit to the camp of the Danes?" the king asked, but this time of asking his voice was apologetic, not accusatory.

"I was a prisoner of the Danes, not their guest. They did not give me tours."

Æthelred nodded, and made an attempt at a smile of placation. "I don't suppose they would."

"No. Nor did you wait upon my prayers before attempting your attack on their camp," I continued. "You wish God's favour, yet do not wait to ask me, God's good man, to make prayer and sacrifice to call his favour down upon you."

The king looked to his brother. "I told you we should have waited until we had offered Mass for our victory."

Alfred nodded. "Mayhap we should. But it seemed to me that we have prayed much, but fought little. I would have us do both."

"As would I," said Æthelred. "But each in their due course. Without God's favour we cannot hope to prevail against this Great Heathen Army that He has sent against us, a scourge for our sins."

"Quite right," I added.

The king turned back to me.

"What is your counsel, holy Bishop Conrad?"

"I would say, let us fall back, to a place secure and with good provisions. The season is bleak, and snow may like enough fall. Let them eat the frost, while we remain full and content and warm within. What say you to that, my lord?"

The king nodded. "That seems good counsel to me. We shall withdraw to our estate at Wellingaford, and there keep watch upon our enemy."

"That is most wise and kingly," I said. "What I would expect from the king of the West Saxons." But before the king could sign his men to begin to fall back, I held up my hand once again.

"Would you have one of your men pick up Brother Odo from the mud? He is rather dirty."

Chapter 18

We retired towards the king's estate at Wellingaford, with me riding Wolfbait and Brother Odo, still dazed by the buffeting he had taken from the king's men, wobbling after me upon Buttercup. It was as well for him the donkey was so solicitous towards him; he would have fallen off any other beast. But I saw the animal skip left, and right, when Brother Odo swayed, and once I swear he turned his head and grabbed him with his teeth as he fell forward.

The West Saxons trudged in the silence of defeat. The king had set a screen of sentries, mounted on horses, behind and around us to watch and warn of any sign of pursuit by the Danes, but the Battle of Readingum had been hard for all; there would be many men, back in the camp of the Danes, with poultices on their heads and blood-stained bandages on their limbs. Our wounded we carried with us, and their suppressed cries and groans were the music of our march. It was as well that there were so few of them, for I could scarce have born such an ill-tuned accompaniment if it were sung by more than the bare handful of men that had been carried alive from the field of slaughter.

Those we had left behind would be silent now, although the ravens would be making their rough music of delight at the blood work of men.

Really, the only joy of riding with a defeated army is the knowledge that you have not been left for the ravens. With the cries of the wounded becoming unendurable to my ears, I decided to ride ahead a way, to see the land where we were heading. To that end, I urged Wolfbait on, and we rode to the front of the column, where the screen of scouts that went before us spread to the left and right of the track. Still, in this cold season, with the trees bare and the bushes naked, and the fields as bare as the table in a pauper's hovel, there was little cover to be had, and less for the sentries to watch for. I drew my cloak tighter around my shoulders, glad for Wolfbait's warmth under my bottom, and saw, from atop the ridge we marched along, the slate grey trail of the river to our right. It ran, broad and sullen, in the low land below this last ridge, turning slowly across our direction of march. The king's estate lay near to the river, upon the shoulder of a gentle hill running down to the Thames.

"It is a cold prospect."

I turned, startled, for I had not heard the approach, to see Alfred beside me, sat upon his horse, his cloak drawn tightly around his shoulders.

I nodded. "It is indeed."

"Made colder by our defeat."

To that I made no answer, for silence better reminded the prince of the counsel I would have given if he had had patience to hear.

Alfred turned to me, his eyes as grey and cold as the river below.

"Such has been the straits of these times that I have taken no chance to ask news of Rome. Is Pope Adrian in good health? By the last letter we received, we learned that he was ailing."

"Oh, he is well," I said, as airily as I might, for I had no knowledge who sat upon the Throne of Peter but only hoped that Alfred had not, either.

"That is well," said Alfred. "For Pope Adrian has always been a friend to us in these islands, holding us dear in his prayers. It would be a great blow if he were to be taken from us and another, less mindful of our tribulations, raised in his place."

"Indeed. He ever spoke of his hopes and prayers for you, my lord."

"For me? I am pleased, but a little surprised, for I had not thought my little fame to have reached the ears of the pope."

"Oh, he has very big ears," I said. "Metaphorically."

Alfred nodded, smiling pleasantly. "The better to hear our prayers. You must have been pleased when he gave you the pallium. To which bishopric are you intended?"

"Oh, Canterbury," I said. I didn't mean to, but it was the only one I could remember when the question came.

"Canterbury? But my brother's namesake, Æthelred, was but recently elevated to the chair at Canterbury and he still lives."

I affected shock at Alfred's words, widening my eyes and opening my mouth. "Surely not?" I shook my head. "But word came, while I was in Rome, of his death. That is why the pope sent me here, to be bishop in his stead."

"In these times, what can men know for certain? But I had words with Archbishop Æthelred but six weeks ago, and letter from him since. If he be dead, he be still fresh in the ground. So where will you take your pallium, Bishop Conrad?"

I shook my head. "I do not know. Mayhap I will return to Rome."

"I do not think that will be necessary. In these times, there are too many bishoprics that lie vacant, without a shepherd to guard the gathered flock. We will find a seat for you, bishop without a see." Alfred glanced at me once more. "But we will needs have another name embroidered upon your pallium. I would see it, that I know how much work it will set the women to stitch it anew."

"Ah," I said. "The pallium. The Danes took it."

"Oh," said Alfred. "That is ill."

"Yes. My men fought for it, giving their lives that it be protected from their heathen profanation, but, like your own men yesterday, they lost."

"And what of your letter of authorisation?"

"The Danes took that, too."

"Dear, dear," said Alfred. "That is ill indeed."

I lifted my hand so that he might see it. "But I have my ring."

"Yes," said Alfred. "So I see." But he looked not upon my ring but on my face, and his eyes were cold. "May I?" He held out his hand to me.

What could I do? He was brother to the king.

The ring slipped off my finger easily enough for my hand was chilled by the wind and I handed it to him. Alfred held it up between us and I saw his eye, looking at me through it. Then, holding it between thumb and forefinger, he slipped it on to his own finger.

"It fits." He held his hand up for me to see.

"Any man might wear the ring, but only a bishop can wield it," I said.

"Indeed," said Alfred, taking the ring from his finger and holding it to me. But as I reached to take it from me, he added, "A *true* bishop."

It was only with difficulty that I resisted the temptation to grab the ring back from him. Instead, I looked to him with all the truth my years of lying might manage and said, "As I am."

I saw his lips twitch upwards in the beginning of a smile but there was no laughter in his eyes. He reached towards me, giving me back the ring.

"It is a precious and holy gift: wear it well."

"I will," I said. "If God give me the strength."

"We shall need all the strength God gives," said Alfred. He turned his horse towards our destination. "Pray we be given it, Bishop Conrad."

"Most certainly, my lord."

I watched him ride to the head of the weary column, and made no effort to follow quickly after.

I feared that the ætheling knew I was no bishop but he had chosen to hold his hand for the while. Now I could not but wonder for how long Alfred would keep his knowledge sheathed, ready to be used against me — and to what end he kept it hidden.

With such dark thoughts rolling through my mind and turning my stomach sour, I finally rejoined the long march of beaten men, back to where we hoped to find safety for some short while against the Great Army.

As I rode alongside the trudging men, their heads sunk down against the wind lash, I thought how the Danes had defeated all the men and armies our people had put up against them. The Northumbrians, the Mercians, the East Angles: kings and thanes and aldermen had met them in open battle, in siege and attempted ambush and in all the six years since the Great Army had landed upon our shores they had not once been defeated.

I would do better to take ship and leave this land while I still might. Mayhap, I thought as I rode, I might ride to where the Narrow Sea separated land from land and find a passage across the grey road. Then the wind lashed my face again, and I knew that in such a season and with the weather so inclement there would be no ships prepared to make the crossing — and nor would I wish to board a boat whose master was willing to put to sea in such conditions.

Unless the winds should change, there would likely be no safe passage until the winter were past, and probably much of spring, too. Mayhap I should seek a different sanctuary, with one of the princes of the Britons who made their homes in the hills and mountains of the west. The tumbling rivers that fell from those hills provided no passage for the dragon boats of the Danes, so they did little but sail past, on their way to the great slave mart at the Black Pool in the land of the Gaels.

Caught up in such dark thoughts, I was content to slip backwards to the rear of the column. There walked the last and the wounded, men making their way to safety with the help of friends and makeshift crutches. Upon Wolfbait, I rode higher than any of them, and could see further, even down to where the river began to roll in a great curve towards the south west. Which was how I was the first to see, in the slant light of the lowering sun, the long shadows cast upon the water by the oars and masts of the ships making their way upstream.

The Danes were coming after us, by river and, turning in my saddle, by land. For in the distance behind, I saw the glint of winter light on a forest of spear tips, raised like a field of metal wheat, marching.

I sighed and turned Wolfbait to the front of the column, where Alfred rode with the king. It seemed my part would be to take them tale of their approaching death. Now if I could but find a way to convince them to send me forth before the battle, I might yet survive the morrow. At the least, maybe there was a way to make it easier for the Danes to kill Alfred. For should he survive the battle then there could be little doubt that the prince would turn his attention to how I had come to acquire a bishop's ring.

I rode up alongside the column, shouting, "Beware, Danes," and pointing to river and land, that all might see their advance and, forgoing hope, turn to thoughts of escape. Indeed, as I passed the men, I saw the whisper fear spread among them, its wings settling over many a turned head. For they had seen and felt the fury of the Northmen themselves all too recently, and knew the tales of their battle prowess to be no mere tales, but true.

They were looking at death, tracking them by land and water.

The more I could make them fear its approach, the better the chance of escaping myself. The king and his brother saw the Danes as God's scourge for our sins and the scandals of his church. But for my part, after my enforced but prolonged contact with the clergy, I had come to the conclusion that most priests and monks were more like Brother Odo than me. There seemed little there that God might wish to punish. No, the reason the Danes had prevailed so often was that they were the most formidable fighting men in our land. For that reason, rather than divine ill will, they had held all the fields of slaughter, while we scurried around trying to amend our lives when what we really needed to do was train our men better and get them better armour. But what king would find armour and spears for anyone outside the band of retainers who keep him upon his throne? Putting weapons into the hands of those not immediately bound to him was simply to store rebellion for the future, when some land hungry thane would promise his churls freedom from their lord's labour if they would fight alongside him. But the Danes shared their weapons among their host, so that every one of them was armed to some degree. Whereas I had seen our men shambling into battle with nothing better than a leather apron and a wooden club. Not surprisingly, such poorly-armed men either fell in the first press of the shield walls or, seeing the well-armed Dane before them, fled before the battle began.

So I rode up the column, yelling, "The Danes, the Danes are coming!" to its head, where the king and his brother had turned to hear what was causing the approaching commotion and spreading ripples of panic through their men.

"The Danes," I added, to make sure they knew who was coming, as I pulled Wolfbait to a halt.

"I think we knew after the fifth repetition," said King Æthelred.

"And we were certain after the tenth," added Alfred.

I ignored their remonstrance and pointed to the river and the approaching column. "They will have caught up with us in two hours," I said. "Unless we scatter. We could split into small bands, each heading in a different direction; they would not split their forces to come after us if we make our escape like that."

In answer, King Æthelred pointed not to where the Danes were coming from but to where we were heading: a scatter of houses and sheds and paddocks around a great hall lying within a great earth bank near to the ford of the river at Wellingaford.

"Then the Danes will take our royal estate at Wellingaford, and all its stores and supplies will be theirs. There is food enough stored to keep their army fed for a month; in which time, they would make such a fortification that we would never be able to shift them, while they would lay waste all this land around — land that is not theirs though they would take it."

I shook my head. "I have seen the Danes, and how they fight. You will not beat them, not with a broken army."

"No," said Alfred, "no we will not. Not on our own. But this time, we will not make the mistake we made before, Bishop Conrad. You will ask God's aid and help before we face them in battle."

"Yes," said Æthelred, before I could think of a good reason why I should not, "and you will accompany me to the field, that you might continue to offer prayers for victory while battle is joined."

"B-b…" I stuttered, but no further words came.

"B-brother Odo?" asked Alfred. "Do not worry, he may assist you in saying Mass."

"No, no," I said, words finally coming. "Where will you fight? There is no good place here — it is open ground and the Danes could outflank you on either side."

But Alfred pointed to the east, where a hill rose over the Icknield Way. "See the lone thorn tree near the top of that hill? From there, we would command the way to Wellingaford and see the ford at Moul, where any reinforcements might land. We should set our men there, for the Danes will not dare march past us. They must needs give battle."

"But if you give them battle, you will lose," I hissed, leaning closer to the king and his brother that I not be overheard.

"That," said the king, "is why we need your prayers. For surely God will listen to the pleas of one of his own bishops."

"And if He does not," said Alfred, "then this land will have no further need of bishops."

Which was how I found myself robing to say Mass in a hastily erected tent under the solitary thorn tree that Alfred had pointed out, growing near the lip of the hill. With a Danish army rapidly approaching, it was a place I would really rather not have been, but the only way to leave was to leap on a horse and ride wildly from the camp. Such a departure would attract attention, and riders sent forth to bring me back. So though my guts and my bowels urged me to fly before the Danes arrived, I tried to ignore their demands — although I could feel and smell the rank fear sweat pricking through the skin — and set to vesting myself with what robes I could find.

Brother Odo, to my annoyance, did not appear to be frightened at all, for he was humming a thoroughly irritating melody, and humming it out of tune at that, while helping me robe for Mass, in between setting up a makeshift altar and gathering the vessels — chalice and paten — required for the saying of Mass.

"Brother Master?" Brother Odo broke off his annoying humming to begin what I suspected would be an even more annoying question.

"Yes?" I said, while struggling to get my cope to lie evenly over my chasuble without disturbing the cassock. Honestly, if I had known how difficult it was to wear episcopal garments I wouldn't have taken them from that dead bishop's boat. But there had been something else, rolled up amid the vestments, that might prove useful should I get away alive.

"Brother Master," Brother Odo repeated.

"What?" The stole appeared to be attempting to throttle me, while the cope had decided to turn into a blindfold.

"Thanks be to God, your plan is working."

"What plan?"

"Your plan, Brother Master. The one to free our brother monks from their slavery to the pagans."

I succeeded in tugging the cope down from my head and getting it round my neck in time to see King Æthelred enter the tent.

"This venerable monk succeeded in fleeing from the Danish camp," said the king. "He has come to us and I have asked him to join his prayers to yours, Bishop Conrad, that we may be granted victory in battle."

The king stepped aside.

"You," said Abbot Flory.

King Æthelred looked to the abbot and then to me. "You know each other?"

Before Abbot Flory could react, I stepped forward and embraced him. "Thanks be to God you have escaped the heathens," I said loudly. "I have prayed every day for your release."

Abbot Flory began to struggle in my grasp.

"Get off me," he said, trying to push me away and turning towards the king. "This man sold me into slavery."

Before I let go of Abbot Flory I whispered into his ear, "I have a pallium and I will use it." Then I stepped back and turned to King Æthelred.

"You sold this holy abbot into slavery?" the king asked.

"Yes," I said.

Æthelred gasped.

"You admit this?"

"I don't just admit it, I *claim* it. Abbot Flory stands with us today because I sold him — it was all part of my plan to save him and the monks of Medeshamstede from the Danes."

"B-by selling us?" spluttered the abbot.

"Yes," I said. "As a slave, you had value to the Danes. As a monk, you had none. Sold, you might be redeemed, or even escape, as you have done — you say." I glanced at the king, for I remembered well his words that treason has ever been the sharpest weapon the Danes wield against us. "But you are with us now, in the hour of our greatest need, and I would ask you, Abbot Flory, to put aside whatever differences we might have had in the past that, together, we might raise our voices in prayer and supplication that victory be granted to King Æthelred."

"B-but, you *sold* me," Abbot Flory spluttered.

"I sold you to save you, and you have been saved," I said. "Now let us join together and offer Mass in thanksgiving and in supplication." I held out my hand to the abbot, as a wise and holy bishop might hold out his hand in forgiveness to one who has wronged him.

Abbot Flory spat on it.

"I will see you hanged," he said, and he turned to the king, his chest heaving in the passion of his hatred, his eyes wild and all but bursting with his anger. I made sure to stand, in contrast, mild and calm and as bishoply as I could be.

"This man, this, this man, he's not even a priest, just a monk, and not long one at that and I only took him into my monastery because his brother brought him to me tied over a horse… and you would listen to him? No, no, give me your sword, your knife even, and I will carve his heart from his chest, if there be a heart there."

As Abbot Flory spoke, his rage overcame him, so that spittle flew from his mouth and his fingernails cut blood crescents into his palms and his hands dripped red on to the earth.

I shook my head, my eyes downcast in sadness.

The abbot stopped speaking, as if struck dumb, his eyes bulging and his throat working.

"It is sad," I said, turning to the king, "how the ill use of the Danes can unhinge a mind, even one as venerable as Abbot Flory's. But he was ever ill disposed towards me and now blames me for the wrath God visited upon the monastery at Medeshamstede; wrath, I might say, occasioned by the way the abbot turned his eye from the impure lives of his monks — why, I told him myself of how one of the brethren was carrying on with nuns and wenches and even the mother abbess of our sister house…"

"One of the brethren?" screamed Abbot Flory. "That was *you*, rutting like a goat rather than living the holy life of the monastery."

I glanced pityingly at the abbot, shaking my head once more. "Is it any wonder God gave his judgement against the monastery, when a man's testimony is turned against him and he is the one accused rather than the fornicating monk?"

King Æthelred, who had been turning from one to the other of us throughout, now looked to the abbot and I saw that the feigned pity I had shown had found a genuine echo in his heart, for he was gazing at Abbot Flory with the sympathy of a man who has discounted the truth of another's words on account of the man's sufferings.

"It is a dreadful thing, to lose that which one loves and to be taken by the Danes," he said. "But I would not hear you cast such calumnies against our dear Bishop Conrad."

"Bishop? Bishop?" cried Abbot Flory, his voice rising in pitch to a shrieking crescendo. "He's not even a priest!"

I shook my head, the sadness in my heart at the breakdown of such a venerable monk apparent for the king to see.

"But he's not," said the abbot. "Have him prove it. Prove it! Prove it!"

I looked to the king and shrugged. "It might help him," I said. "Once he was a good and holy abbot." And I slowly raised my hand so that the winter sun glinted on the ring upon my finger.

Abbot Flory gaped at the sight of the ring. Wearing it, I ranked as far above an abbot as an abbot stood over one of his monks.

"No," whispered Abbot Flory, "no, it can't be. Not you. Not *you*." He looked up from the ring into my face.

I answered, without sound, my lips forming the shape of the words, "Yes, me."

If it hadn't been for the prospect that I might shortly die, this would have been the most enjoyable day I could remember since finding myself trussed over a horse and delivered to the monastery.

I turned to King Æthelred. "You will have more important things to do than wait upon a bishop struggling with his vestments, so I will send Brother Odo to call you when I am ready."

"Brother Odo!" Abbot Flory, hearing his name, looked round wildly until he saw the monk, as self-effacing as ever, standing in a fold of the tent. The abbot ran to him and pulled Brother Odo out of hiding, placing him in front of the king and I.

"He will vouch for the truth of what I say," said Abbot Flory, "for I know Brother Odo to be a monk who speaks only the truth."

I saw, by the blood rushing to Brother Odo's cheeks, that he was all too conscious of the sudden scrutiny of so many great and powerful men. His mouth opened and closed again, but no sound came from it.

My day was in peril of becoming as bad as any of the others since I had fled the Danes with the Book in my possession.

King Æthelred looked to the blushing monk.

"It seems that all agree as to the truth telling of your tongue. So, speak. I command it."

Brother Odo looked around with all the panic of a cornered deer. Fortunately, everyone was looking at him, or they might have seen that I was just as panicked.

"Er, what do you want me to say?" asked Brother Odo.

"The truth," said the king.

"The truth?" asked Brother Odo.

"Yes," said Æthelred. "What else?"

Brother Odo opened his mouth, closed it again, his eyes flicking from me to the abbot and back again, while I mouthed to him, "Say nothing," and Abbot Flory tried to tell him what to say. King Æthelred, hearing the abbot, shook his head and held a finger to his lips.

"Shh," he said. "Let him speak the truth."

But still Brother Odo could speak no words, although his mouth moved.

"The truth," said Alfred, coming in to the tent, "is that the Danes will be upon us within the hour and we must make our prayer for victory now or we shall surely fall before them."

Brother Odo pointed at the prince. "Y-yes. That is the truth. That."

"But…" began Abbot Flory.

"Here," I said, passing him my cope. "Put this on. We will make the sacrifice of Mass together."

Abbot Flory looked at me. He was about to refuse when Æthelred said, with all the brittle confidence of a man lately defeated, "God will surely hear the prayer of a bishop and an abbot. Quick, begin the Mass."

The abbot looked at me. If he had had the power to kill by thought, I should have been lying cold upon the floor. But neither words nor thoughts will kill a man, but the steel and iron that will was approaching fast. I leaned towards him.

"The Danes will kill us all. We will settle matters between us afterwards; for now let us pray for victory."

Abbot Flory could see the approaching Danes as well, and he had the more recent experience of them. From the way he paled at the sight of the two approaching columns of men, the memory was ill. He whispered to me. "But you are not ordained, you cannot say Mass. You don't even know how."

"I do," I said. "A lot has happened in the last weeks, including my ordination and elevation to the episcopate. But since it's all happened so quickly, I might need a little help with the Latin. We'll have our backs to them." I glanced at where Æthelred and Alfred were vesting themselves, in the manner of kings and princes: padded vests, mail shirts, leather gloves. "They won't notice if you whisper what I have to say."

"God will," said Abbot Flory. "I should denounce you."

"You already have," I said. "They believe me, not you. Do you want to waste the time we have left before the Danes arrive?"

"God will not hear a prayer offered up from an unclean heart."

"He's not listened to any of the prayers from clean hearts like yours," I said, as I finished vesting myself, "so let's try one from me."

I turned to face the king and his brother, and their immediate retainers gathered behind them. The rest of the men were waiting outside the rude tent that had been fashioned for the saying of Mass, split into two shield walls. Because of the slope, and the lip of the hill, I thought it likely that the Danes could see only the first of the two groups, with the second concealed by the flattening of the ridge to the hill top. As I spread my arms to begin the Mass, my mind wandered as it always did at such times, and I thought as to the name of the hill where we stood. I suspected that, whatever its previous name, it would acquire a new one by the end of the day and I feared that it might be named King's Fall.

But seeing the array of faces turned towards me, faces of hope and fear, of doubt and anticipation, I found the words that I needed to say.

"In nomine Patris, et Filii, et Spiritus Sancti…"

Unfortunately, once the Mass began, I had to turn round, to face east. Which meant that I was looking in the same direction as the congregation, towards the approaching Danes.

It is as well that most of the Mass is said quietly, for the sight of an approaching army has the effect of drying the throat and stealing the voice.

I could see them, split into two columns, with one climbing up on to Moulsford Hill across the valley from where we waited, while the other marched towards us along the old path, the Icknield Way. The men marching straight towards us came with a banner flying in front of them, but in the dead calm of the morning the banner hung limply from the standard, so I could not see who led them. To my eyes, it seemed that the second army, having climbed to the top of Moulsford Hill, was seeking to make their way down from its other flank to come round on the other side of us. I suddenly realised, in the midst of asking the Lamb of God to have mercy on us and to take away our sins, that they were aiming to catch and crush us between the two arms of their army.

As I realised this, the standard bearer at the front of the army coming straight towards us started to wave the banner, pulling it out through the air so that all might see who marched behind it. To my horror, I saw that they marched behind the Raven banner. One of the sons of Ragnarr led the Danes.

From the whispers spreading behind me, I realised that I was not alone in seeing the banner, nor in discerning the strategy of the Danes. Then whispers turned into hurried movements, and I realised that men were moving into position, while quiet orders were being given. I felt my chest draw tighter and those familiar cold hands working their way into my bowels.

From where he was standing beside me, I could see Abbot Flory had also heard the movement behind us, and by the ashen colour of his face I knew that he was no more keen to be around when battle commenced than I was. I had to finish the mass as quickly as possible, so that I would have a chance to get away before the battle began in earnest.

It's remarkable how quickly you can say the Mass if you try. In less time than it took for the Danish army to advance a hundred yards, I had galloped through the gradual, sailed by the sequence and gabbled the Gospel. But in saying the Gospel, I had to turn my back on the Danes and face my anxious congregation, with all eyes looking past me to the advancing army. Ending the Gospel, I reduced the sermon to a quick, a *very* quick prayer for victory but as I ended that, I saw King Æthelred make his way towards me.

"Be quick," he whispered. "I may not leave to face the enemy until Mass is over."

"I will," I said.

"Then you will stand beside me as we face the Danes," he added.

"Pardon?"

The king fetched me a brief smile. "I can see, from the speed at which you are saying the Mass, that you are as eager to face the Danes as I. I will not gainsay your wish."

With that, the king knelt again, while I felt the fear fingers, which had loosened slightly as I reckoned that there would be plenty of time for me to escape after finishing the Mass, tighten again at the realisation that Æthelred expected me to stand with his personal retainers, calling out prayers and psalms as men were screaming and dying all around.

I slowed down. Where before I had been gabbling through the Mass, now I began to intone it, slowly and sonorously, rolling the Latin vowels over my tongue. Well, I would have rolled them, only my throat was so dry that the sounds came out as cracked as old wood. Abbot Flory, hearing the change, looked to me and I saw that the fear that had previously gripped his face had gone, to be replaced by the resolution of a man who has decided to face battle bravely and to die a martyr if necessary.

"Why have you slowed down?" the abbot whispered.

"We must say the Mass properly if God is to hear it," I whispered back, in between my long-drawn out phrases. I wondered if I might sing the Mass to draw it out even longer, but I did not know it well enough for that, and what I could not risk was the king realising that this was, in fact, the first time I had ever said Mass.

Behind me, I could hear further whispered conversations as the realisation slowly dawned that the Mass was taking longer than expected. Indeed, an advantage, I realised, of the whispered words of prayer was that I could hear other whispers behind me and, in particular, those of the king and his brother.

"They are trying to flank us," I heard Alfred say.

Indeed, he did not need to say it, for I could see it for myself. The second Danish column, the one that had climbed laboriously to the top of Moulsdown Hill, was now making quick time along the ridge. Should they just follow the lie of the land, they would soon come level with us, and then only a shallow dell separated them from where we were arrayed, around the solitary thorn tree.

"Can you stop them?" Æthelred asked him, while I intoned the Canon, stretching out the syllables until they barely met.

Behind me, I could feel eyes measuring times and distances and numbers of men.

"Yes. But I will have to go very soon," said Alfred.

"I will wait for the other column here; let them come up to me, where we have the advantage."

"Pray for me, brother."

"I will hear the Mass for both of us," said the king.

Then, from the sounds of movement and the clink of mail, I knew that Alfred and his men were withdrawing from the tent and moving to where his command waited.

As I moved, at the pace of fog, through the Mass, I heard the sound of orders given and the shuffle of many feet making their way towards the enemy, and from the corner of my eye, as I continued my slow progress through the Canon, I could see Alfred leading his men towards the flanking column of Danes.

For as long as he might, Alfred kept his men concealed, using the ridge as cover by marching his men beneath its lip. From where I stood, it seemed the Danes had not realised that Alfred was approaching, for they were still running in swift but loose formation along the rise.

"Get them, Alfred, get them."

I was not the only one watching. Æthelred's attention was as divided as mine, although with somewhat more excuse, given that it was I that was saying Mass and he was simply hearing it.

Looking down into the valley before us, I saw that the Danes were slowly forming up at the bottom of the rise. They could see us, waiting at the top of the hill, and knew well that we had the advantage of the ground. But with the expectation that their other wing would attack us from the flank, the Danish force that followed behind the Raven banner lined up into the shield wall. Although they were below us, yet they were a formidable sight, for every man that I could see was dressed in mail armour, and many had helmets, while there were as many swords as spears bristling from behind the line of shields, each painted with some savage device.

The army we faced had taken its fill from the weapons and armour of three kingdoms. In comparison, of the men that Æthelred could call upon, only his own household retainers were armed to match the Norse. The rest, the men called from their fields and homes to defend them, had mostly no more protection than a shield and a leather cap, while for weapons there were many spears but precious few swords, and far too many clubs and sickles and hammers. They were farmers, not warriors, and only fear for their families and sworn oaths tied them, for the moment, to following the king into battle. Should the battle turn ill, or the king fall, then they would surely flee, as the dogs of fear and panic were loosed.

"Hurry, please."

I had not heard the king's approach, but now he stood at my shoulder, looking past me at the men massing at the bottom of the hill.

"I — I must ask the saints for their aid and protection," I said. For I had come to the litany, that part of the Mass where we call upon the dead to aid the living.

"St Peter…"

"…pray for us." The king finished.

"St James and St John…"

"…pray for us."

At the familiar recitation, I felt the fear fingers loosen once more, for there are a lot of saints one might call upon — and I intended to call upon them all. For surely, once Alfred loosed his attack upon the other wing of the Danish army, the men in front of us would have to go to their aid, lest their own flank be destroyed and they be laid open to a devastating attack from the side.

"St Alban…"

"…pray for us."

"St Aidan, pray for us."

I had stopped waiting for the response, for every man in the congregation was looking to the right, where Alfred had drawn up his men in silence, waiting for the Danes to pass before charging down upon them.

"St Edwin, pray for us."

But the Danes stopped at a shout of command. I saw a scout sent ahead, moving towards the ridge. They suspected something.

"St Oswald, pray for us."

Alfred did not give the scout the chance to discover the trap: he sprang it. With a great shout, Alfred led his men over the lip of the hill and towards the Danes. If they had only come on a little further, the charge would have taken the Danes in the flank and they would surely have been scattered but now Alfred's men had to charge along the hill to meet the Danes.

There was reason the Norsemen had laid waste to our kingdoms, and I saw the reason then.

"St Cuthbert, pray for us."

Despite the surprise, the Danes deployed into line more quickly than I had ever seen men move, but even so, Alfred caught them before the line had chance to tighten into wall — and the wall broke.

With his men around him, Alfred broke into the centre of the Danish line.

"St Chad, pray for us."

He was going to win the battle for us while I prayed!

"Hallelujah, St Michael, pray for us!"

"He's doing it," whispered Æthelred.

"St Gabriel, pray for us."

But the Danes were all hardened warriors, while our men were not. Though the centre of their shield wall had broken, the flanks had not, and they began to push aside the farmers and peasants standing and waving their spears at them, and close in around Alfred and his household warriors.

"Hurry, hurry," said the king, "finish the Mass. We must go to him."

That was where Æthelred made his mistake. If only he had not said, 'We must go to him.' The fear fingers gripped once more and my mind skated through justifications for why we could not move, settling upon the words in front of me.

"I must finish calling on the saints to aid us," I said.

"Hurry, then, *hurry*," said the king.

So I sped up, but it's remarkable how many saints you can call to mind when you really need to. There's St Januarius and St Lawdog and…

"St Gall, pray for us."

"You're making him up." Abbot Flory looked sharply at me.

"No, I'm not," I whispered back, in between responses. "Patron saint of chickens."

"Hurry up," said Abbot Flory. "The Danes are advancing."

He was right, they were. But, to my immense relief, they were not advancing up the hill towards us. Rather, seeing the battle on their flank, the Raven banner of the sons of Ragnarr had turned from its intended path. They were going to crash into Alfred's men, before they had the chance to overwhelm the left flank of the Danes. For while I had been running through saints, real and imaginary, Alfred's men had rallied, the farmers had remembered their homes and their wives and their children, and pushed back upon the Danes that were attempting to encircle Alfred, so that now they were fighting to their rear as well as their front.

At the centre of the chaotically pushing and shoving mêlée, the golden wyvern of the West Saxons, Alfred's standard, was raised high. He was doing fine on his own. He certainly did not need me to risk my life on his behalf.

Besides, I still had a long way to go before finishing the litany of the saints and we would need the help of all of them.

"St Severian, pray for us."

"You really are making them up now," said Abbot Flory.

"Martyr," I replied. "St Bru, pray for us."

"Oh, come on," said Abbot Flory.

"Iron faith," I said.

I felt a hand on my shoulder, and a mouth whispered into my ear.

"Since you are so keen to invoke every saint, you will lead us into battle, calling on the saints as we go." The king stood beside me, his sword in his hand.

"L-lord, I am a man of peace."

"Good. You will carry no weapon — your prayers will be our shield."

"Er, maybe I could have some armour?"

"I have none to spare." Æthelred turned to his men. "Quick. My brother needs our aid. Let us give it to him."

The men streamed from the tent, calling orders and arranging the line, while I stood, staring in horror down into the valley. Already, the Raven banner was half way to where Alfred stood at bay. The Danes were advancing quietly, without their usual battle cries, for they wished to fall upon the flank of Alfred's army with as much surprise as they might muster.

"Aren't you going to warn them?" I asked Æthelred.

But the king shook his head. "Alfred is the lure to draw the hawk down from its perch. Let it stoop, and catch its prey." Æthelred looked at me. "You have put up a hawk? Once it has its prey in its claws, it will not drop it, even if that means it cannot fly. So I will stoop upon the grounded hawk, and the hunter will become the hunted."

But already the Raven banner closed upon Alfred's men, and the grim sword work was begun. The farmers, beset in turn from behind, began to break, and flee, and the Danes set up a great shout.

"You'd better hurry," I said. "Alfred won't hold for long now."

"He'll hold long enough," said Æthelred. He turned to me and a grim smile was on his face. "At least for me."

Brotherly love among princes. Few survived it. As the Danes broke upon his men, I doubted that Alfred would.

"St Tron, pray for us."

The king stopped in the act of pulling down his helmet. "*Now* you're making them up."

"Bishop and abbot," I said. "St Thecla, pray for us."

"Surely not."

"Virgin and martyr."

"Let's hope she prays hard and God hears her prayer," said the king. "Or you'll join her as martyr." He looked at me. "Although probably not as virgin. Let us go."

So, with me beside the king, we began to advance upon the maelstrom of blood and metal that swirled around Alfred's banner. I looked to see if I could change places with Abbot Flory, but the monk was rushing as enthusiastically towards the battle as any of the warriors, his face suffused with the unearthly light of a man who no longer fears death. My face, I knew, would be reflecting no such light.

"Pray!" shouted the king. "Pray!"

I tried, oh, how I tried to fall back, to let the eager warriors around me surge past, so that I might gradually drift towards the back, but so eager were Æthelred's men and so tightly were they pressed together that the only way I could have fallen back was by falling over, and then I would have been trampled to death beneath their feet. So, instead, I stumbled onwards towards my death, with the gorge rising in my throat and the fear acid swirling in my stomach. It was only a question of whether I would throw up before I died or afterwards. Did dead men vomit? I'd seen them spew blood often enough, why not vomit?

"St Bairfhion, pray for us."

There is one area, and one area alone, where my fear comes in useful during times of danger. For most men, when they panic, become blind and unthinking. Whereas when I panic, my eyes see more clearly and my mind becomes more active, seeking some way to save myself. So as we charged towards the swirling, chaotic battle, I saw that the Danes had become almost fully engaged, with few held back in reserve. Admittedly, those of Alfred's men not actually fighting were either dead or running, but enough remained to keep the Danes occupied, so that only their meagre reserve turned to meet Æthelred's charge.

Gibbering out my prayers, I charged with the rest of Æthelred's men, although for the final few paces before the dreadful clash I was held up by the press of men around me, my feet moving in the air without touching ground.

Near to me, I heard Æthelred put up his battle cry and an answering cry rose up from Alfred's beleaguered men as the crash came, pitching the king's army into the flank of the Danish forces.

For a moment it seemed that they would crack and break, but the Danes held, men holding to each other as men do aboard a boat when the waves threaten to pull them over the side, and the battle turned into the murderous hacking, thrashing scrum of screaming warriors and dying men that all battles, in my far too extensive experience, devolve into. I've heard scops sing songs of the glory of battle, of courage and duty and faithfulness to death, but I've seen what really goes on, and it's all about fortune and luck, and the slip of a foot on bloody grass or the head turn when a spear flies past.

In the mêlée, unarmed and as frightened as it is possible to be and still retain some ability to move, I shrieked and dodged, trying to avoid the knots of struggling men falling towards me while looking for the currents of battle to open up a clear channel, that I might escape from the midst of the battle. But whenever a way opened and I moved towards it, another group of hacking, fighting men would block it, and I was pushed back into the centre of the fight. For fight it was. Warriors and scops like to dignify such struggles by calling them battles, but this was a fight, with as little art to it as two boys struggling and punching and biting each other on the ground, and indeed, I saw many such fights, with men rolling over each other and reduced to using teeth and nails for the loss of their other weapons.

It was one of those rolling balls of death that made me step back and, in stepping back, I tripped over a man whom, I saw in my falling, was kneeling down. If there is one thing worse than kneeling on a battlefield, it's lying down on it, for both leave you helpless and unable to move. I fell among the dead and, in my panic, flailed amid the stench and slipperiness of spilled entrails and burst bowels, unable to get back to my feet, until I felt hands pulling me upright.

"Brother Master, are you all right?"

I suddenly realised who the man kneeling down in the middle of a battlefield was.

"What the Hell are you doing here?" I asked.

"Praying," Brother Odo replied, as if it was the most obvious answer in the world. I suppose it was, for him.

"You!"

The scream cut through the clang of metal on metal and the cries of the dying and the shouts of the victors. It cut through the noise because it was directed at me. I turned to see a vision that seemed to rise from the bowels of Hell. A man, if he was still a man, painted red with blood, his own blood and the blood of his enemies, advancing upon me with his sword drawn and murder in his eyes.

Earl Thorgrim.

Brushing aside men with his shield, he paced towards me, his eyes as red as his sword, and I saw that his sword dripped gore. The earl had killed many men during the course of this battle, and he was about to kill me.

I could not move. When faced with death advancing towards me, normally my legs act by their own will and take me as far and as quickly away from it as possible. But here, my legs froze. I could not move them, not under Thorgrim's death stare, even when I tried to pick up my thigh with my hands and shift it. I was like the chicken, held immobile by the line in the dirt drawn from its beak, as the axe hovers above its neck.

But, unlike the chicken, I knew I was about to die and I felt the fear gorge roil in my stomach and rise in my throat.

Thorgrim paced death towards me and it was as if all the other men on the battlefield, all those fighting and dying warriors, had been veiled from sight and hearing. All I saw was the earl and all I heard was the hiss of his breathing and the chink of his mail as he pulled back his sword to ready it for the thrust that would skewer my guts and spill my steaming entrails on the blood-slicked grass.

When the thrust came and I looked down, surprised, as all men are to see what was inside spilling to the outside, I knew that I would scream louder than a pig being slaughtered. There would be no dignity in my death, no nobility or grace or courage. I would die blubbering in pain, trying desperately to shove my entrails back inside my body.

Thorgrim stabbed me.

But as the sword stabbed forward, Brother Odo leaped in front of me, and the sword struck into him. He fell, wrenching the sword from the surprised hand of Earl Thorgrim.

I looked into the earl's face, and my poor stomach finally gave up its contents in one single convulsive, projectile vomit. The acid stream splashed into his face, steaming and stripping the blood from it and leaving the earl clean of blood but covered in bile and, suddenly, momentarily, blind.

Thorgrim raised his hand to wipe his eyes clean but as he did so, I saw something bright and shiny emerge from his chest.

Still blind from my vomit, Thorgrim never saw the blade that killed him. As swiftly as it had pierced him, it was withdrawn, and Thorgrim fell, landing on the prone body of Brother Odo.

Where Thorgrim had so recently stood I saw Alfred, the killing sword in his hand. He, seeing me, said.

"You distracted him long enough for me to kill him."

I nodded.

My mouth did not seem to be working at the moment.

Alfred nodded down at my feet.

"Greater love…" he began.

I nodded; I knew the rest of the quote.

Then Alfred, his household troops thick about him, turned away, ready to plunge afresh into the fray.

But already the word was beginning to spread among the Danes that Thorgrim had fallen — being so tall, he was easily seen and thus readily missed — and some among them began to fall back, eyes searching to left and right for ways from the battle.

Alfred, seeing the hesitation spread among the Danes, turned back to me, a wolfish grin upon his face, and said, "They falter! Now to make them fail." Raising his sword, he screamed the battle cry of the West Saxons and, forming his men once more into line, charged downhill to where the Danes were attempting to reform, around the Raven banner of the sons of Ragnarr.

The crash of their onset was like the sound you hear when a man, reaching from a ladder to fix the thatch of his house, overbalances and falls to the ground: the thud of flesh on earth, with an overlay of clashing metal. But more than anything, it was the sound of weight, of men putting all their strength into breaking through the Danish shield wall.

And it broke. Before the onslaught, men fell and were trampled underfoot. Others, pulled from their shield mate, began to back away, and then backing away became turning away, which was followed by running away.

The Danes were breaking.

For my part, I had more important things to do. For lying at my feet was a dead Danish earl and no one around to dispute with me as to who should relieve him of the wealth he carried. I knew well that no Dane would ever trust his gold with any other man, but would carry it with him, in the finery he wore and in the weapons he bore. I bent down and felt at Thorgrim's waist. Yes, there, in the pouch he wore upon his belt.

It was satisfyingly heavy in my hand as I lifted it, but I was sure that an earl such as Thorgrim would have more. The problem was, he was lying rather awkwardly atop Brother Odo. To check the body better, I had to move him, so that I could roll him over, front, back and side. Bending down, I hauled him off Brother Odo, the earl's legs dragging Brother Odo over himself, so that he lay upon his back, staring up at the sky. His eyes were open, in the way typical of men newly dead, as if they were staring in surprise at something they had not expected to see.

What was not so typical was the way the eyes blinked.

I was busy pulling off Thorgrim's mail shirt, so the movement was only a blur in the corner of my eye. I stopped, but Brother Odo made no other move, so I shook my head — the fear of battle and the relief of living was making me see things — and went back to stripping off the mail. The gold Thorgrim had in his belt was what he would give to retainers, to men who had fought bravely in battle and warranted reward but under the mail was where he would keep his own gold, close to his skin.

But if I could dismiss Brother Odo blinking as a sign of my own relief, I could not similarly dismiss the sound, and sight, of him coughing.

"What are you doing alive?" I asked Brother Odo. Not that the fact of his being alive was of any great moment to me, but the custom on a battlefield was that the man who brought down another was entitled to strip him of his wealth. Alfred was busy elsewhere, and being a prince of the West Saxons, he claimed a share of the overall battle spoils. But Brother Odo could lay claim to Earl Thorgrim's portable wealth alongside me, as we both had reason to say that we had played our parts in his demise: me, by vomiting in his face and blinding him and Brother Odo by saving me and taking the earl's sword out of the battle for a crucial few moments.

Brother Odo sat up, blinking in that thoroughly stupid way of his, as if he found the world and its ugliness a perpetual surprise.

"Brother Master," he said, seeing me, and his expression of bovine stupidity turned into an equally bovine one of joy, "you are alive." He looked down at Earl Thorgrim. "He is dead."

"You do have a gift for stating the obvious, Brother Odo. Do you remember aught of what happened in the last few minutes?"

Brother Odo shook his head. "No."

"Well, let me remind you of how you were about to be killed by the Earl, but I pushed you out of the way, saving you, and then slew the earl myself."

"You did?" asked Brother Odo, eyes wide with wonder.

"Yes. So, naturally, I claim the spoil."

"Of course," said Brother Odo, as I bent to the search once more, finding almost at once a hidden pouch in the earl's jerkin. "The widows and orphans of the men slain here will thank you for your kindness, Brother Master, but I know you would eschew their thanks, so great is your heart."

"Yes, yes," I muttered, finding some hard little objects sewn into the lining of the earl's cloak: jewels no doubt.

"You might eschew their thanks, but I will ensure they give it."

I looked up, with an awful sick feeling in my stomach, and saw Alfred standing over me, his hand held out.

Around us, the battle was all but over. The remnant of the Danish force was streaming away down the hill, a tight knot of men holding fast around the Raven banner and fighting their way back to the river, while others trusted to their own flight and were cut down. Men were sitting and staring up at the sky they had not expected to see again, others lay exhausted in the field, while those who had stood back from the battle now moved forward to claim the dead and strip the bodies.

Alfred waggled his fingers and, affecting a joy that I certainly did not feel, I handed over the purse.

"Many widows and orphans will have the pain of their loss eased by your great generosity," he said, holding his other hand out. I went to take it, only to realise that Alfred was not offering a hand to me, but to Brother Odo.

"I would know how you still live, Brother Odo," he said. "That sword thrust would have skewered a wild boar."

Brother Odo shyly pulled down his tunic to reveal a second, iron skin. "I — I thought to put on a mail shirt," he said, blushing. Turning to me, he said, "I beg your forgiveness, Brother Master. I have not the great faith and trust in the Lord you have, for you went on to the field of slaughter with only your prayers to protect you, where I, lacking your faith, put on this borrowed armour."

"You have both rendered us great service this day," said Alfred. "We would give reward but," and here he looked on me with an expression that told he suspected I might not be as I would appear, "gold, to those so holy as you, is scant reward. We will offer prayers, and praise, and thanksgiving!"

I tried to smile. I really did try to smile. But then I remembered the Book, that I had carried through flight and fear, through trudge and cold, and the ring I bore upon my finger. Though I had, perforce, to give Thorgrim's gold to widows and orphans, as bishop I would have manors and villages and maids, all given to my keeping — not to mention the Book that I would put in my minster church, drawing the pilgrims to its call. For it was, after all, a miraculous Book: one that had escaped the pagan Danes and brought about their downfall.

Unfortunately, I was not the only one to remember it.

"Where is my Book?"

I did not need to turn round to know the voice.

"Abbot Flory," I said. "You too have lived to see our victory. I am so pleased."

"Yes, I am alive, with no thanks to you, and I want my Book back." The abbot looked to Alfred. "I want this man condemned for pretending to be a bishop when he is no more than a monk."

"Are you not a monk too?" asked Alfred.

But before Abbot Flory could find his voice through his spluttering, the king made his way to where we stood, with his most loyal retainers at his side — the others were busy plundering the corpses that littered the hillside.

"You live, brother," said Æthelred, clapping Alfred on the shoulder. "So we can celebrate my victory together."

"I think I played some small part in it," said Alfred.

"As did all who fought here. Indeed, for a while I was not sure how it would go; I even took a wound myself but I see you are untouched."

"Are you badly hurt?" asked Alfred.

"A cut, nothing more," said Æthelred. "It will heal. Unlike the Danes that lie scattered about."

"But the son of Ragnarr who lead the army has escaped."

Æthelred shook his head. "It does not matter. After such a beating, I doubt he will try his luck again." The king turned to where the rest of us stood, waiting upon his word. "But now, we have a matter to settle. For surely the prayers of these religious called down Heaven's favour so that we enjoy victory. However, now we must learn the truth. Brother Odo, speak. Which of these men," and the king pointed to me and Abbot Flory, "speaks truly?"

This was it. It was all up. Brother Odo always spoke the truth. He would tell the king and Alfred that I was impersonating a bishop, and they would inflict some dreadful punishment upon me.

Brother Odo looked to the king. "What shall the penalty be for he who has not told the truth?"

Æthelred looked to his brother, then to the rest of us. There was all too much amusement in his eyes.

"The penalty should match the gravity of the sin. If the abbot has born false witness against this good bishop, then he must make proper penance before God and his fellows. I will leave divine retribution to those who interpret God's writ, but before his fellows let him bear thirty stripes."

At this, Abbot Flory gasped. "Thirty?"

The king looked to him. "Too few?"

"No, not at all." The abbot pointed to me. "What of him? He is the liar."

Æthelred nodded. "If he is indeed the liar, then it is true: there can be few sins worse than claiming the mandate of God's holy church when you do not have it. What do you say, brother?"

Alfred nodded. "Yes, brother."

"For such a sin is treason against God, his church and me. For that, he would hang."

I was going to die. And there was nothing I could do about it.

Æthelred looked to Brother Odo once more.

"Think well on this then, Brother Odo. Which of these men tells truly, and which lies."

Brother Odo made no reply, but looked from me to Abbot Flory and back again.

"What are you waiting for?" said Abbot Flory. "Answer, and we can go back to the monastery."

Still Brother Odo said nothing.

"Oh, come on," said Abbot Flory.

"If you cannot speak, then point to he who speaks the truth," said Alfred.

Slowly, Brother Odo raised his hand and pointed a shaking finger. At me.

"What?" Abbot Flory shook his head. "No. No! That cannot be. I am telling the truth, he is the liar, they are both liars, he has infected Brother Odo with his deceits…"

"Take him away," said Æthelred to his men. "We will think on what further punishment to inflict upon him later."

"Perhaps," I suggested, as Æthelred's men dragged the protesting abbot away, "you might sell him into slavery. After all, that's what he said I did to him. Why not make it true?"

"Indeed," said the king. "That strikes me as most fitting. What do you say, Alfred?"

"I say," and Alfred looked searchingly at me, "I say that we should make a thank offering for our victory, something truly worthy."

"Oh, yes," I said. Thank offerings normally came to the bishop offering them; I'd see that some of the offering stayed with me.

"Something like the Book you have brought to us," said Alfred. "Let us give it, in gift and thanksgiving, to the Pope in Rome."

"The Pope?" I spluttered.

"A splendid idea," said Æthelred. "A true token of our thankfulness."

"Give away the Book?"

"Or would you rather we sent it back to Medeshamstede, the monastery whence it came?"

"But it wouldn't be safe there, not with the Danes so close."

"Indeed," said Alfred. "I fear nowhere is safe while the Danes sail their ships around our coast. Therefore, send it to Rome, in gratitude for our deliverance, where the Holy Book will be safe. What do you say?"

There wasn't anything I could say. Maybe a mother, seeing her only child torn from her and taken into slavery, might feel as bereft, but I doubted it. A woman can always have another child; I could not get another Book.

But as a holy and truthful bishop, I could not but accede, and in good grace, to the king's command.

"Brother Odo, bring the Book and lay it before the king, that he might decide whether he would, in truth, send it away." I hoped that the seeing of it might light the king's gold lust, or his desire for beauty, or the vanity that saw kings acquire the unique for their own keeping. Brother Odo, silent as death and near as pale after seeing his testimony lead to Abbot Flory being dragged away, went to fetch the Book. Looking after him, I spared a thought for why he gave the truth to me.

Must have been because he believed me.

God, I was convincing. Even though Brother Odo must have known that Abbot Flory was telling the truth, and I lying, yet having been my servant these past few weeks, he had come to believe me.

I was so good, I almost believed myself.

Epilogue

That, I thought, was that.

The Danes defeated, Abbot Flory sold off, again, into slavery, and me, gifted with a quiet little bishopric. Alfred had taken me aside, a couple of days after the battle when the ravens were still picking the last scraps from the Danish corpses we had left on the hillside, and explained that, while the Pope may have given me the pallium of an archbishop, it must have been in error. Archbishop Æthelred remained stubbornly alive and was showing no sign of going the way of all flesh. But, if I were minded, he would find me a bishopric.

"I could have use for a man like you," said Alfred.

"In what way?" I asked.

"It may be that, in these fraught and dangerous days, I might perforce have to take the throne. There are those who might question how it is that the youngest of five brothers should become king. Base and false rumours, of course, but you know how it is: rumours fly while the truth is stumbling around trying to find the door to the stable. A man of wit and subtlety, and one set in authority, skilled in words and their meaning could do me great service in such circumstances."

"Where exactly was this bishopric you mentioned?" I asked.

"A quiet one." Alfred looked at me searchingly. "One as far from the Danes as may be in these times."

I nodded. "I should like that. I have had my fill of the Danes."

Alfred laughed. "As have we all."

Which was how I found myself riding with Brother Odo through the cold of a winter's morning to my new bishopric. Where it was, and of my life there, I shall tell in future, should there be people wishing to hear my tale, but there is one matter that I would speak of before I end the story of how I became the most unlikely of bishops: how it was that Brother Odo spoke the truth of me over Abbot Flory.

For myself, I had given it no thought but on our journey west I was wakened on the first night by the sound of leather on flesh. I sat up from where I slept by the fire to see Brother Odo, stripped to the waist, whipping himself until the weals bled red upon his back.

I would have fallen back to sleep if I had been able, for I had heard that some men were wont to enjoy the chastening of leather, although usually at the hands of some doxy, but the sound of leather, and the constant undertow of muttering from Brother Odo, kept me from sleep.

"Oh, for goodness sake," I said. "If you must pleasure yourself, do so away from me, so I can sleep."

Brother Odo stopped and looked to me.

"Do your father and mother yet live, Brother Master?"

"That bastard? For my blessing, he died five years back. My mother I never knew: she died birthing me and my brother. But my stepmother, the Lady Godgifu, now *she* was a woman I honour."

"Because she looked after you as a mother?" asked Brother Odo.

"Not exactly as a mother." I grinned in happy memory, while Brother Odo blushed red.

"Why would you know these things?" I asked.

221

Brother Odo answered my question with another, even odder. "But you are not married, are you, Brother Master?"

"Married? Of course I'm married. That's why I ended up in the monastery. My wife cuckolded me with my own twin brother, then vouched for him as me and I was tried for the crime of tupping my own wife!" I looked at him. "Why do you ask now?"

But Brother Odo shook his head, muttering to himself, "That is all ten then."

"All ten of what?" I asked.

He looked up at me. "The Commandments. I thought you might honour your father and your mother and if you weren't married then you couldn't have committed adultery. But that makes it all ten."

I shook my head. "What do you mean?"

"With adultery and dishonouring your parents, you have broken all ten of God's commandments."

This was not quite what I had expected to hear from Brother Odo. "If that's what you think, and personally I would say that while I might have bent some of them, I certainly haven't broken all ten, then why did you tell the king that it was me who was telling the truth?"

Brother Odo stared at me, his eyes wide in the firelight. "When King Æthelred said what the punishment would be if he found out that you had lied, I knew already that you had broken eight of God's commandments and that in condemning you I would also be condemning you to Hell. So, God help me, I said that Abbot Flory lied, for his punishment chastises only his body; it does not ruin his soul. By my lie, you live, and may seek forgiveness. But now I know you have broken all ten commandments." Brother Odo picked up his whip again. "I lied, that you might live and find repentance, and this is my penance for sinning against the truth and Abbot Flory." And he began to flay himself once more, setting to with grim determination.

I sighed. "If you must," I said, and settled to sleep, drifting off to the regular thwack of leather on flesh, and Brother Odo's whimpers of pain.

Historical Note

So, is it true? The honest question of the child when told a tale is, at heart, the same question that springs in the heart of the adult reading historical fiction — and it lies at the core of what the writer is doing. For the answer, for any good piece of historical fiction, to that question must be, "Yes." It is true, insofar as the author is capable of making it true and, what's more, it is true in two different and sometimes conflicting ways. Being anchored in history, it should cleave to the historical record: the writer should knowingly introduce nothing false and, by his research, ensure that he does not unwittingly write in anachronisms of fact or, harder to eliminate, attitude. But, being historical fiction, for the book to work it must also answer to the stringent demands of storytelling: it should begin, middle and end, with people who are true as characters, in the time and setting that they are inhabiting.

So, is it true?

Mostly.

As you'll know, having come so far in the company of Conrad, truth for him is a slippery concept, and one employed to his own advantage. As the writer of his adventures, I follow his example, squeezing the truth until it begs for mercy and then smoothing it into story. So

Medeshamstede Abbey, which was re-founded in the later tenth century as Peterborough Abbey, where we first meet this most reluctant monk, was sacked by Viking raiders some time during the depredations of the Great Heathen Army. The exact date is uncertain, however, so it could have happened at any time during these turbulent years. As for Conrad, would a nobleman who had become an obstacle to the plans of his fraternal rival and unfaithful wife have been unloaded into a monastery? Possibly. It was certainly the fate of a number of noble women, whose husbands had died and who did not wish to be forced to remarry, or whose families decided it were better to marry them to the Church than into an allied clan. For such women, it was not a bad choice at all, giving them considerable autonomy within the structures of the church. At this time, younger sons were sometimes earmarked for a clerical career from an early age, and it's quite likely that Alfred himself, as the youngest of five brothers, was meant to go into the Church. But as his elder brothers died off that possibility receded, until by the start of this story, as the only brother of the reigning King of Wessex, he was required to marry and prepare himself for rule.

So, it is possible that Conrad could have been carried, all unwilling, into holy orders, there to make his escape when the Great Army came calling. The Gospel Book that is the great treasure of the monastery I have based upon one of the surviving Gospel Books from Anglo-Saxon England — the Barberini Gospels. This beautiful book has been kept in the Vatican Library since 1902 and, while scholars are still unsure of its provenance, it seems to have been the work of three or four different hands, at least one of which was from Mercia. With Medeshamstede being one of the most important monasteries in Mercia, I have appropriated it for the story.

Gospel Books such as the Barberini Gospels, as the physical

embodiments of God's truth, were richly decorated both within, in terms of the pictures and ornaments and the words on the page, and without, where the book's covers were studded with jewels and bound with gold: the physical manifestation of the glory within. Such a Book would, indeed, have been a treasure worth saving and, in Conrad's case, profiting from. He would not necessarily have had to despoil the book to profit from it: the Codex Aureus, a Gospel Book now kept in the National Library of Stockholm, bears this inscription in its margin:

Ic Ælfred aldormon ond Werburg min gefera begetan ðas bec æt hæthnum herge mid uncre clæne feo; thæt thonne wæs mid clæne golde…

I, ealdorman Ælfred and Werburg my wife obtained these books from the heathen army with our pure money, that was with pure gold…

Books were precious. With the Gospel Book in his possession, Conrad could both gain entry into any royal or ecclesiastical establishment, but also turn a pretty profit. But there were easier ways to make money in the ninth century…

The taking and selling of slaves was a key aspect of the Early Medieval economy with the Vikings the pivotal slave-takers and slave traders. Archaeologists have found, mute but telling, the iron neck collars that Viking slave traders used to tie their human wares together and bring them to market. At this time, there were few settlements that rose to the status of a 'town', although London had become known as the pre-eminent place for the buying and selling of imported goods. Most markets were seasonal and those dealing in imported items were often littoral, with sea traders pulling their boats up on to a gently sloping and protected beach to sell wares from Christendom and beyond. In return, the traders bought furs and, the most valuable export of Britain, dogs and slaves. British hunting dogs were renowned throughout Europe; British slaves were not regarded quite as highly as British dogs, but they

EDOARDO ALBERT

were valuable nonetheless. Most of Conrad's fellow monks would have ended up exported along the network of trading routes that used the North and Irish seas, and the Channel, as shifting silver highways: the sea, for all its dangers, was nevertheless usually safer and almost always swifter than the laborious land routes.

But Conrad could not be satisfied with the profits from his slaving venture; the Gospel Book had stoked the gold lust in his heart and, pursuing it, he arrived at the town that would later come to be called Bury St Edmunds — but obviously had not yet acquired its new name. And this is one of the points at which a historical novelist faces a historical dilemma: Edmund did not die in Bury St Edmunds. His body was translated there once a suitable shrine to the martyr king had been built. But as to where he actually did die, no one is sure. A number of possible locations have been proposed, but none are completely satisfactory. So, for simplicity's sake, and since *Beodricesworth* doesn't have any modern associations, I've placed his death at the site of his final resting place.

However, Edmund was indeed king of the East Angles, and the Great Army had first landed in his realm and remained there for a year, amassing men and material for its assault on the kingdoms of the Anglo-Saxons. But Ivarr, Ubba and Halfdan, the leaders of the army, had left Edmund upon his throne during this time. It was only on their return, having conquered Northumbria and subdued Mercia, that they moved against the East Angles. As to what exactly happened, the *Anglo-Saxon Chronicle* laconically states that:

In this year the army rode over Mercia into East Anglia, and there fixed their winter-quarters at Thetford. And that winter King Edmund fought with them; but the Danes gained the victory, and slew the king, and conquered all that land.

Not much to mark the passing of one of the four great Anglo-Saxon kingdoms. But a century later, around AD 985, a monk named Abbo of the monastery at Fleury in present-day Saint-Benoît-sur-Loire in France wrote an account of the Passion of St Edmund, noting in his dedication that he learned the details of the story from Dunstan, Archbishop of Canterbury, who himself averred that he had been told what had happened by Edmund's armour bearer. It is from Abbo that we learn how Edmund challenged Ivarr to embrace his faith in return for his kingdom, and how Ivarr responded by having his men throw so many spears into the king that he seemed more hedgehog than human being, and yet still lived.

Whether Abbo's account is accurate or not (and most scholars are willing to grant it a general veracity), what is undeniable is that, a generation after his death, the children of the men who had killed Edmund were venerating him as a saint and his shrine in the renamed Bury St Edmunds had become a bustling centre for pilgrimage. The sacrifice of the king proved, in the end, more enduring than the spears of the men who had killed him.

For Conrad, this was all in the future. He was still on the run and, running, he was dragged down into the cave dug under Rohesia's Cross. The modern name for the town is Royston and the cave, shaped like a fat bottle, is still there, underneath the crossroads at the centre of the town, one of the most enduring mysteries in England. For the cave was rediscovered in August 1742, but despite the best efforts of historians, they have found absolutely no record of it before that. Unfortunately, the spoil within Royston Cave was removed in the eighteenth century, so there is no way of establishing when the cave was dug. The only clue lies in the mysterious carvings that line its walls. Most scholars think the cave was dug sometime in the High Middle Ages, but some investigators put its excavation back into the Early Medieval period and that's what I've used for the purposes of the story. Royston Cave is open to visitors on Saturdays and Sundays between Easter and October for a small entrance charge: if you can, try to see it.

As for Conrad's eventual meeting with Prince Alfred, there is nothing in the historical record — a record that was largely written at the behest of the eventual King Alfred — to suggest that Alfred ever met an itinerant monk under such circumstances. But the story of the desperate battles waged by Alfred and his brother against the Viking attack on their kingdom is accurate, and one that Alfred evidently recounted to people later in life, as his biographer, Asser, tells how the king himself showed him the solitary thorn tree around which the battle of Ashdown swirled. Asser tells us that Alfred engaged the enemy while his brother, King Æthelred, remained at his prayers, not willing to start the battle until the Mass he was hearing was over. While it was certainly true that combatants at this time looked to divine help as much as earthly arms, it seems unlikely that a warrior king would risk losing a battle in such a way: it is more likely that Alfred and Æthelred had agreed a strategy where Alfred would be the bait, drawing the Danes on and engaging them until Æthelred slammed into them with his own troops. Whatever the real reason for Æthelred's delay, his arrival was enough to ensure a significant victory for the men of Wessex, the first that had been won against the Great Heathen Army. In the story, Conrad finds himself the unwitting architect of this strategy of delay, for which he gains much credit from Alfred.

The Battle of Ashdown was followed by a number of other engagements through that long winter, all of which the men of Wessex lost, but in none of which were the Vikings able to win a sufficiently crushing victory to force the capitulation of the kingdom. But they did gain one significant triumph: sometime not long after Easter 871, King

Æthelred died, from causes unspecified in our sources: it could have been infection from battle wounds, disease contracted in one of the many temporary camps where his men bivouacked during the conflict, or a winter accident. Whatever the cause, Alfred, the youngest of five brothers, now found himself King of Wessex. As for the Vikings, this struggle was proving bloodier and far less profitable than an army of professional plunderers would wish: they put out feelers and Alfred answered: it suited both parties to end the conflict through payment, rather than by blood. Alfred bought peace — for a time. As for Conrad and Brother Odo, their adventures will continue through the fraught decades that follow, when an England that did not yet exist hovered on the brink of being aborted before it could be brought to being.

CPSIA information can be obtained
at www.ICGtesting.com
Printed in the USA
FSHW021957020620
70853FS

9 781839 011627